BETSY

A Sweet Romantic Comedy

SARAH MONZON

RADIANTPUBLICATIONS

Manuscript edited by Katie Donovan

1
Betsy

"If you get your mouth any closer to that mic, it's going to file sexual harassment charges against you." I sat back from my own mic with a huff, clicking off the intercom that allowed Tate to hear me in the sound booth. The kid was okay. Mostly. He could go from needing his ego stroked one minute to being a pompous butthead the next, but he paid me upfront, so that was a point in his favor. He also caressed the snot out of the microphone stand and was better at looking like he was making out with the equipment than singing on key.

But hey, who was I to crush his dreams? I'd leave that up to people like Simon Cowell while collecting the recording and editing fees Tate racked up. I may've had the overwhelming urge to take a long, scalding shower after each of his sessions, but at least I could afford my water and electricity thanks to him and other wannabe hopefuls.

"How was it that time, Betsy?" He looked through the glass separating us, his eyes wide with anticipation and endless aspirations. Ego-stroking moment. Got it.

My friends called me a cynic. Claimed I was trilingual—fluent in English, Spanish, but mostly chose to converse in sarcasm. They weren't wrong. But I also wasn't needlessly heartless.

I leaned toward the mic next to the control panel and flipped the switch so he'd be able to hear me. "Better than last time, Tate." Last time I swore the ally cat whom I'd taken to calling Mr. Whiskers and who loved to feast on Mr. Chen's leftover sushi had screeched and hissed in protest. "You're really improving." He couldn't have gotten any worse.

Tate pulled at his shirt collar, preening at what he considered words of praise.

Should I have felt bad for giving him—and pretty much eighty percent of the aspiring musicians that booked my services—false hope? Maybe. Then again, there were plenty of people in this world that loved to put others in their place and rip the glittering curtain of their longed-for future down to reveal the stark reality for what it was. So if anyone claimed that letting Tate and others like him live in their happy, if delusional, fantasy a little longer was unkind, well, I'd argue the opposite.

"Should we go through the song one more time?"

Tate asked as he grabbed the mic stand and pulled it so close he practically straddled the metal pole.

I winced but forced a smile. "I think you've got it as good as it's going to get."

He beamed, thinking I meant that he and the song couldn't get any better because he'd already reached perfection level. See? Happy fantasy land.

I'd yet to run into a musician that was even halfway in touch with reality. Malachi's brother came close, but then, he'd almost literally risked the farm for his big break, not unlike Jack and his handful of magical beans. But in the case of Malachi's brother there hadn't been a golden goose at the other end of the beanstalk.

Tate ran a finger along the body of the microphone, like a lover reluctant to leave and needing one final lingering caress. His lips moved in a silent whisper, and I was glad I'd turned off the feed so I couldn't hear whatever sweet yet disturbing nothings he whispered into the windscreen.

Every surface in that room was getting Lysoled as soon as he left.

The door to the sound booth finally opened, and Tate stepped out. "When do you think you'll have the single edited and produced? I have some leads I want to follow up on. I can feel it, Betsy. My big break is just around the corner."

The only break for Tate, around the corner or otherwise, was the shattering of his dreams to be on the radio and have a platinum record. "I'll email you the file in a couple of days."

He nodded, and I expected him to say something else that reeked of overconfidence and self-import. Instead, he didn't make a move except to slide his hands into the front pockets of his low-riding jeans.

I bit back my sigh. "Is there anything else you need?" *Don't do it*, I pleaded with him in my mind, even though I knew he'd ignore my warning, spoken or otherwise.

Musicians were like that. Plowing ahead. Thinking other people were beneath them, that rules and boundaries applied to everyone *but* them. The only thing they cared about was making it big and then making it even bigger.

Somewhere, my brain registered the vulnerability in the way Tate shifted his weight from one foot to the other. How his gaze darted about the room before settling back on me. Instead of seeing his boy-band blue eyes, I saw unsettling brown ones instead. A familiar unease churned in my chest, and my palm flew up to stop him before he ever managed to get a word out.

"Do you remember my rule?"

The vulnerability, which I now saw had only been an act, vanished from his face. His jaw set in a stubborn line, and his chin jutted out. "Rules are meant to be broken."

I didn't know if I felt more like sighing from the

onslaught of exhaustion that came over me or screaming from sheer frustration.

If only my soul didn't find its freedom in music. If only my heart didn't beat to the rhythm of a drum or my blood flow on the strums of a guitar. Then I wouldn't have to deal with musicians and their kind.

Tate took my silence as an invitation and stepped closer. A cocky smolder I didn't doubt he practiced for hours in the mirror made his lips twist in a disturbing way. His hand lifted, but my reflexes batted his sticky fingers before they could touch me. This time when his eyes widened, it wasn't with hope but outrage.

I longed to take a step back but instead lifted my chin. I wouldn't give up ground. Wouldn't make a move that resembled retreat. "I have one rule and one rule only: I do not, under any circumstances and with zero exceptions, date musicians."

Tate pursed his lips but then shuffled back a step. Then another. "Fine. Your loss." He stalked to the door and ripped it open but paused before making a dramatic exit. He looked at me, and this time his top lip curled. "You would have been nothing but dead weight anyway. You're not even that hot."

I gripped my chest as if wounded. "Oh no. A man-child without enough talent to fill a thimble thinks I'm not that hot. Whatever will I do?" I rolled my eyes and planted my hands on my hips. "I'm pretty sure I'll live."

He called me a name that started with the second letter of the alphabet and rhymed with someone whose favorite mode of transportation was a broom before storming off down the street.

Good riddance.

I grabbed the can of disinfectant from under the bathroom sink and marched toward the sound booth like an armed assailant. Maybe I'd douse myself while I was at it. I did feel rather germy.

I retrieved my wireless earbuds from my pocket and placed the speakers in my ears. I needed a reset. A reminder of why I was in this industry in the first place.

I needed the music. Unadulterated. Pure.

A few swipes of my phone and a solo guitar alternating the arpeggiated chords of C major and A minor —the intro of "Hallelujah"—tunneled its way through my ear canal to that place deep within me that music alone could touch. Everything calmed. The air, my breath. My eyes slid shut and my lungs expanded. Everything that had felt wrong suddenly felt right.

No one was in the studio, so it was safe. To not hold back. To let the music in. To let it fill me and then release it back into the world again on the strands of my vocal cords. I let the music move me. Feel me. Change me. Then I put all the emotion and heart the composition had collected into each of the lyrics. Into every rise and every fall. Until I felt equally spent and revived by the last *hallelujah*.

The silence cracked with the sound of applause. I whipped around, my pulse pounding like a taiko drum, the reverberation ripples of adrenaline coursing through my system. I held the can of Lysol out in front of me, my finger on the trigger.

A man stood just inside the door. He'd been smiling when I first turned, but now his face froze as he eyed me and my germophobic weapon.

That's right. Be afraid. I have an aerosol spray can, and I'll use it in a heartbeat.

"Who are you and what do you want?" I closed one eye and peered down the barrel of the jet stream.

He looked dangerous. Not in the *I'm robbing you, give me all your money* sense, but in the way his grin lifted slightly higher on the left, the lopsidedness instantly disarming. Or the way his eyes had a calmness about them. They could easily lure an unsuspecting woman in and then convince her of anything.

My grip on the can tightened.

"My name is Asher North." His voice reached across the room and enveloped me like a warm blanket.

One I immediately shrugged off.

If I'd had spidey-sense, it would have been tingling right then. All my intuition said to stay on guard. This guy was hazardous, to me specifically. Not my physical person—I lowered the Lysol can—but he could hurt me in ways that sometimes never healed.

"If you're selling something, I'm not buying." I gave him a look that had sent more-hardened guys running the other direction.

"You have a beautiful singing voice," he said like I

wasn't glaring a hole in the middle of his chest. He shook his head in amazement. "I've never heard anything like it. The way you…" His voice trailed off, his head shaking again like he couldn't come up with a few adjectives to describe how I sounded.

I stared at him. I was sure he expected me to thank him for the compliment, but it was more likely we'd see snow here in Southern California in July before that happened.

He lowered his hands slowly, and I noticed the closely trimmed nails and calluses on his fingertips. A guitarist.

"Do you sing in a band?" His voice was doing that reaching thing again.

I crossed my arms over my chest. "No."

"Solo artist?"

"No."

"But you are a professional singer." He said it so matter-of-factly. As if any other conclusion would be out of the question.

I smiled. "No."

He stilled. Not that he'd been moving in the first place. This was different. I wasn't sure I would have even noticed except for his sudden change. There was an energy about him. Maybe how his voice seemed to move the air particles in the room. How the timbre could reach inside a person and stir something deep within them too. Probably what made me wary about him in the first place. But now that the energy wasn't moving, a desperation began to claw at my center. The stillness was almost more than I could take.

Then he blinked. His grin returned.

I let out a long exhale. Just as I'd known what Tate would say before he said it, I knew what the next words out of this Asher North's mouth would be.

"No." I cut him off.

His brows furrowed. "But I haven't even said anything."

I shrugged. "You were going to say something pretentious. Offer me the opportunity of a lifetime." *Your sarcasm's showing.* I could hear my friend Nicole's voice in my head. "Tell me how you can make all my dreams come true." I snorted. "I'm a sound engineer, not a singer, so unless you need to produce a recording or hire a professional at your next live performance, then like I said, I'm not buying what you're selling."

His every blink was a staccato beat. I could almost hear the crescendo of his thoughts as they built behind his frozen expression. A rest. Then he's pianissimo again, soft and calm.

"As a matter of fact, I could use an audio engineer."

Suspicion crept up my spine. "Oh, really?"

He nodded and looked around the studio. I followed his gaze. The lobby was small, but what did he expect? All the magic happened in the two rooms behind me. This space held little more than a couple of chairs, a small side table, some posters of some of my favorite legends—Aretha Franklin, Roy Orbison, John Lennon—and metal die cuts of the bass and treble clefs.

"Why else would I be here?" His eyes held mine. Not in challenge like I would've done, but in a silent assurance that I could trust him.

I swallowed back my derision. His Y chromosome made him unlikely to be trusted, but the fact he was a musician guaranteed there was no chance whatsoever.

"Uh-huh." I turned to put back the Lysol can. I had better things I could be doing.

"Wait."

I looked over my shoulder, and the persistent nuisance had walked halfway across the room to intercept me.

"I'm not sure what I did or said to get on your bad side."

I let the silence stretch before replying. "I don't have a bad side."

His brows rose. "This is your good side?"

My lips curled. "I only have one side."

"Right. Okay." He nodded in agreement like I made perfect sense.

I bit back my grin.

"Can we start over?" He took another step forward and held out his hand, his lopsided, disarming smile steady on his face. "I'm Asher North, lead singer and guitarist for the worship band True North. We're going on tour in two weeks and are in need of an audio engineer to head up the sound at each of our venues."

I eyed him from the top of his curly brown hair that looked to have wrestled free from whatever product he'd used that morning to tame it, all the way down to his scuffed low tops. My gaze snagged on his proffered hand. Even when he'd been on the other side of the room he'd felt too close. Dangerous. You didn't put your hand where a snake could strike it.

As if sensing my resistance, he teased, "I promise I won't bite."

I pumped his hand once, then let it go. "Worship band. Like Hillsong United?"

"Something like that, yeah."

"And you're only looking for a sound engineer? Nothing else?"

He hesitated.

"I'm assuming since you're the lead singer of a worship band that you're a Christian, so I don't need to remind you of the ten commandments. Especially number nine that says something against telling lies." I raised an eyebrow.

He huffed, and it sounded like half a groan and half a laugh. "Your voice—"

"Is not singing on stage," I finished his sentence. I looked at him again. Behind the calm in his eyes, I sensed a deep determination. If I agreed to go on tour with his band as his audio person, he wouldn't be satisfied. He'd keep strumming this chord—me singing with them in front of the audience—until the strings broke.

And that was never going to happen.

"I'm sorry, but I decline your offer." I made to turn, but a warm hand on my arm stopped me. I whirled around, my movement knocking his hand away. "Don't touch me."

His palms rose in the air, his eyes wide and an apology on his lips. "I'm sorry. Would you at least think about it though?" He pulled his wallet out of his back pocket and retrieved a small rectangular piece of paper. "I'm going to leave you my card. It has my number on it." He leaned over to place the card on the small round table, then picked up a pen and wrote on the back of his card. "I never said how much we could pay. I've put the amount there, on the back, in case you're interested." He walked backward to the door, his stupid grin in place. "It was nice to meet you, woman whose voice is going to haunt my dreams tonight."

I didn't want to be any musician's dream girl, but before I could tell him my name in hopes of not being a personal nighttime ghost, he was gone.

My gaze slid to the white slip of paper on the table. Curiosity nudged me the few steps until I stared down at it. I should've picked it up and thrown it in the trash. Instead, I flipped it over really quickly, as if his writing would've burned my fingers if I'd lingered.

The number written in a bold hand caused me to suck in my breath. *¡Ay, caray!* That changed everything.

2
Asher

*T*he sanctuary at Grace Chapel echoed my footsteps as I made my way down the center aisle to the stage. The acoustics in the large room had the ability to pick up the barest of sounds and magnify them like an amplifier. Which wasn't forgiving when a note hadn't been hit just right or Jimmy came in half a second too late on the keyboard. A good reason why it was the perfect place to practice. Making a joyful noise unto the Lord was all well and good ninety-nine percent of the time, but when the group played for more than an audience of One, they needed the noise to sound more like magic.

The afternoon sun streamed through the large west-facing stained-glass window behind the stage, casting a brilliance of kaleidoscopic colors along the polished wood floor. This was my favorite time of day to practice because of the light. The visual display helped remind me of how the light illuminates, both physically and spiritually.

"Any luck?" Dave, our drummer, entered from a side door, his drumsticks in hand. I swore he slept with the two pieces of wood under his pillow. No one ever saw him without them. Usually, the drumsticks hitched a ride in his back pocket, but the closer we came to the first concert of the tour, the more his fingers fiddled with the B sticks.

I jumped onto the stage, watched the colors bathe my skin, then walked to my guitar case. Ever since hearing that woman's enchanting voice, my hands had itched to feel strings beneath my fingers. Notes danced in my head, playing tag with each other, so far refusing to be caught. There was a song there. I could feel it. I just needed more...

The locks on the guitar case released with a click. I lifted the hand-crafted instrument up by the neck and settled the construction-worker-orange strap over my shoulder. Closing my eyes, I took in a deep breath and placed the tips of my fingers on the strings along the fingerboard.

"Hey, Asher." Dave's shrill whistle nearly pierced my eardrum as it expanded with the acoustics, chasing the notes that had been playing in my head completely away.

I sighed and rested my hand on the smooth body of my Martin.

"I asked if you had any luck," he repeated.

Luck had nothing to do with anything. No, what I'd had this afternoon was wholly Providential. I fully and completely believed God had directed my steps into Seventh Street Sounds at that exact moment. What I'd heard was a gift. And a shame. Because no light as bright as hers should ever be hidden. It should be shared with the world. It should shine for all to see, illuminating the darkest of places and starting other flames blazing as well.

But how could a wildfire spread if the source insisted on staying contained?

"What's up?" Tricia asked somewhere behind me.

I hadn't even realized she was there. Had she been there when I came in, or had I missed her entrance?

"Asher's all up in his head again," Dave replied, a short quality to his voice.

He was a talented drummer. Hit and kept the beat perfectly. But he played the notes and not the other way around. He didn't surrender to the music. Let it consume him. And he didn't understand those who did.

"Is he writing another song?" Tricia asked Dave, not bothering to direct her question to me. We'd been playing together long enough for them to know that if music was speaking to me, then that's all I'd be able to hear in the moment, no matter how much she said or how loudly she said it.

Clothes rustled, and I imagined Dave shrugging his wide shoulders. "Beats me. But we have a lot of details to bang out and confirm before the tour, so we need his head here, not in the clouds."

I strummed a G-major chord. "I'm here, Dave."

"Finally," he muttered.

I switched to a C-major chord as I turned. Jimmy, our keyboardist, should be arriving any minute along with his teenage son, Marcus, who played bass. Then we could start practice. "To answer your question, I found more than I was looking for."

Dave stopped twirling his drumsticks. "Can you be any more cryptic?"

Tricia supported her expanding midsection with one hand, her other absently stroking circles on the side of her belly. One thing was for certain, that baby would never suffer not knowing it was loved a single day of its life.

"What do you mean, Asher?" she asked.

I played a I-V-vi-IV chord progression, my fingers finding the correct strings with the same precision of a dancer landing on their mark. "I found us a sound engineer who can also step in to the role of lead female vocalist if…" My voice trailed off as I looked at Tricia.

Tricia sighed. "I've told you a thousand times. The baby and I will be completely fine."

I nodded to let her know I'd heard her, even though I wasn't convinced, then repeated the progression. "Only problem is, she didn't agree to take on either job."

"So you've got nothing and we're still down essential people to make this whole tour work. Great." Dave rounded the drums and sat down heavily on his throne.

"I've got conviction." I hummed a measure of one of our more popular songs. "I left her my card with an offer on it. Don't worry. She'll call."

"Sorry we're late." Jimmy burst through the sanctuary doors like a locomotive full of steam, Marcus on his heels.

"You didn't miss anything." Dave tapped his drumsticks along the edge of the hi-hat cymbal.

Jimmy took his place behind the Yamaha keyboard set up to the right while Marcus plugged his bass into the amplifier.

"Let's start with 'My Maker and My King.'" I faced the empty rows of seats and imagined them filled with people wanting to lift their hearts to Jesus in praise.

Jimmy played the solo intro on the keyboard. On the third measure, I picked up the tune by plucking arpeggiated chords. Dave and Marcus came in on the fifth measure along with Tricia's mezzo-soprano voice rising above all the instruments:

"My Maker and my King,

All praise to You we sing.

Seated on Your throne above,

We lift our hearts to You in love."

In harmony, I blended my voice with hers for the next set of lyrics.

"My Father and my Lord,

Your grace on us You've poured.

Unworthy though we are,

You heal our wounds and bear our scars."

Marcus hit two consecutive wrong notes. He tried to correct, but everything was off, and one by one we stopped playing our instruments.

"Sorry, guys." He didn't look any of us in the eye. "My bad."

"It's okay," I said. "Let's do it again from the top."

We played through the song twice more without a hitch. As the music washed over me, I could feel my center align. Things that had seemed so big and insurmountable before faded into the background.

This. Always this.

I prayed. Went to church. Read my Bible. But I never felt so connected to my Savior as when I lifted up my heart in song to Him. If ever my eye turned away from the Source of my praise and I sought to use my God-given gift for self-gain instead of as an offering to the Lord, then I prayed He'd take my voice away from me.

A hiss, then a groan sounded to my right, pulling me back from the intimate place I went when in song. Tricia's shoulders hunched as she clutched her rounded belly.

In a fluid motion, I spun my guitar behind my back and raced to her side. "Are you okay?"

Jimmy reached her next from the other side, a cell phone already in his hands. "Who should I call?"

Tricia's face pinched, but she put out a stopping hand. "No need to bother anyone," she panted. After a second, she paused then straightened. "It was just Braxton-Hicks."

"What's that?" Marcus hadn't budged except to use his guitar as a shield. As an only child, he probably hadn't had much experience being around pregnant women.

Tricia gave him a reassuring smile. "It's my body's way of getting ready for the baby. Practice round, in a sense."

His young face scrunched, but then he shrugged his narrow shoulders and pulled his phone out of his back pocket and starting messing with it.

"Why don't we take a break," I offered. Braxton-Hicks may've been natural, but they still looked like they hurt.

Tricia stretched her back. "I could sit for a minute or two, thanks. My feet have been killing me lately."

I reached for her hand to help her off the stage, but she shooed me away. "I'm pregnant, not an invalid."

Even so. "I'm going to find you a stool or something to sit on. We'll add that to our supply list for the tour, too." I hopped off the stage and marched toward the side exit. The church had a storage room where they kept extra chairs and things. Maybe I could find a stool there.

The storage room was down in the basement beside the fellowship hall where they had potlucks and social functions and even wedding receptions when a couple booked the church as a venue. Growing up a Christian, I'd walked into my fair share of churches. They all had a very similar smell, especially in the lower levels. Years' worth of reheated home-cooked culinary dish aromas had seeped into the walls along with an undertone of dirty diaper stench from the nursery and the smell of stale coffee from the large urns that served congregants alongside boxes of donuts before services. Grace Chapel, with its fresh paint, new carpets, and modern seats instead of pews, wasn't exempt from church basement smells.

I fished out the keys from my pocket and unlocked the door. Wedged back in a dark corner, past stacks of extra chairs and a plywood cutout nativity, was a slightly wobbly stool. I hauled it out, knocking over a stack of dusty hymnals with one of the feet. The top book fell open, the notes on the pages drawing me in. I couldn't *not* stop to thumb through the compositions. That would be like asking a reader to not pick up a book when they were at the library. Or an athlete to not touch a ball on the playing field.

Some people thought hymns were outdated, but I tended to see them as classics. Songs like "Amazing Grace" and "It Is Well" still had the ability to move people to tears hundreds of years later. The power of music was timeless.

I only let myself look at a couple of songs before I righted the tumbled stack and locked the storage room back up. When I got back to the sanctuary, Dave and Tricia were staring at each other in a silent standoff.

"What's going on?" I asked as I approached with caution.

Tricia rose from the seat slowly, leading with her middle as if hoping to get the extra weight there to a certain point so gravity would take over and help her right herself the rest of the way. "In case none of you numbskulls heard me before, let me say it again. As a member of True North, I will be going on this tour. The baby isn't due for another six weeks. If there comes a point when I think I need to step aside for any reason, then *I* will make that call. Got it?"

Dave huffed before stalking back to the drums without either argument or acquiescence. Jimmy saluted while Marcus froze as if any tiny movement would alert the predator to his location.

Tricia took the stool from my hand, climbed onto the stage, and set the seat where she'd been standing during practice earlier. She perched on the edge. "Good. Now. That being said, I also think it's time to add another female to our group." She turned her hawk eyes on me. "What do you say, band leader?"

I grinned. I could already picture Seventh Street girl up on the stage with us. Her riotous curls a halo of personality in the spotlight shining down from the rafters. Her earthy, rich voice blending with my deeper, even tones to create a euphonic experience. "I'm already on it."

I just had to convince her to stop hiding her light under a bushel and let it shine, let it shine, let it shine.

3
Betsy

One question bounced around in my head as I drove to Nicole's house. Should I tell my friends about Asher North's job proposition or not? I already knew what they'd say. That I was crazy for not accepting on the spot, especially after seeing how many place values were in his offer. And my family could really use the money. We'd all been saving for a family-based green card for my *prima* Camilla. Tia Alma and Tio Sergio had been granted permanent resident cards along with their two younger children, but Camilla had turned twenty-one a month before, so she'd no longer been eligible to immigrate with her family. The limited number of slots available for the second preference category—the one she fell under—meant the wait could be long, but we couldn't even start the process without the funds for legal and filing fees.

On the other hand, there was my rule. Which my

friends knew about, but not why. And even though Asher North had been totally professional and hadn't hit on me or made any moves that would break my no-dating-musicians policy, I couldn't help but be cautious. He had a glint in his eye that made me uncomfortable. A spark that said he knew how to push boundaries to make them wider so he never actually stepped over any line. I didn't trust him.

And worse—for some reason, I didn't trust myself around him.

Which left me in this predicament. Should I sell out for the sake of my family and put myself in a situation that could lead to untold troubles, or should I—

Wait. What was I saying? What was I *thinking*? This was *la familia*. You did anything and everything for family. I'd just have to put on a second layer of sarcasm armor and make sure Asher knew that no meant no. I would *not* be singing with him and his band. Period. I'd manage their audio and equipment and make sure they sounded the best they could. My job description in highlights, bold, and italics. End of story.

I parked on the street in front of Nicole's house. Even if I'd never been to her charming bungalow before, I'd have known which residence belonged to her. It was the only one where the sod had been ripped out and raised gardens installed in neat little rows. I'd made the mistake of commenting on her landscaping choices the first time I'd visited and had to endure an hour lecture on the substantial harm lawns did to the environment with the waste of water, the gas it took to mow the grass, and the millions of pounds of pesticides used every year.

I should have known better than to ask or comment. Everything was a cause with Nicole. Totally annoying but also endearing, because how could you stay upset with someone who cared so much? And she did care. About everything and everyone. Honestly, it was a little exhausting to be around, so usually I countered her soapbox rants with a well-placed quip.

Besides Nicole's electric car with the *Save the chubby unicorns* sticker on the bumper, two trucks and a minivan also occupied the drive and curb by her house. The men must not have wanted to be separated from their ladies. I wasn't sure how I felt about that. On the one hand, part of me missed the days the five of us would huddle in Molly and Jocelyn's living room, sipping mocktails and pretending to sew. Or at least Amanda, Nicole, and I pretended. Molly and Jocelyn actually created some pretty amazing pieces. Then again, the appearance of my friends' significant others had had a balancing effect on their sometimes over-the-top personalities.

Molly still held strong to her strict honesty policy, but since meeting and marrying Ben, she'd learned to temper the truth with a healthy dose of common sense and graceful tact. Jocelyn had found the courage and security in Malachi's love to finally follow a life dream that she had buried deep under Excel spreadsheets and financial analysis reports. Drew had opened Nicole's eyes to the importance of not taking everything so seriously and the truth that a little fun in life was also worth fighting for. Finally, Amanda...well, without Peter, Amanda would probably still be suffering silently with the symptoms of her undiagnosed autoimmune disorder, still refusing to let her friends and those who loved her support her.

All of my closest friends had been hit hard by Cupid's arrow. I was happy for them. But if that flying diaper baby even so much as thought of practicing his archery skills by using me as a target, I'd hunt him down and do more than just clip his wings. I wasn't above the threat of bodily harm. Even on mythical creatures. Just saying.

I liked my single status. I didn't have to deal with someone putting demands on me, or divide my time and focus to accommodate a fragile male ego. Honestly, relationships looked like little reward for a whole lot of effort. I'd pass on that cruise ship, thank you very much.

I grabbed my grocery bag of ingredients—reusable canvas so I wouldn't have to see Nicole's reproving look or hear the statistic on how many plastic bags ended up in the oceans every year (yes, avoiding lectures was a highly motivating reason to do or not do something)—and hauled myself out of my beat-up thirty-year-old Toyota Corolla. The car was like an old vinyl record—some scratches here and there, lots of crackles and pop sounds, and occasionally getting stuck and needing a swift kick in the pants to get started again.

Since it looked like all the guys were in attendance, I was glad I'd bought two two-liter bottles of ginger ale instead of just one. I'd have to slice the pint of fresh strawberries I'd picked up at the roadside stand a little thinner, though, to make them stretch for eight drinks.

The front door swung open with a turn of the handle. Voices and laughter drifted from the great room at the back of the house as I toed off my shoes and padded my way to the kitchen, my socks slipping a bit on the bamboo hardwood floors.

"Betsy's here!" Amanda shouted from her place on the corner of the couch. Her legs were tucked up underneath her, and she snuggled into the broad side of her NFL-star fiancé.

"Practicing for your cheerleading tryouts?" I raised a brow at her enthusiasm. I'd arrived, not won the Superbowl. No need to celebrate to that decibel.

Peter wrapped his oversized muscled arms around Amanda. The man could plow down quarterbacks like a semi over a bicycle, but the way he touched Amanda, he might as well have been wearing kid gloves and handling a priceless treasure. He pressed a kiss to her temple. "She's my favorite cheerleader."

I rolled my eyes and looked to Molly, thinking she'd be the most likely person to agree that the mush factor with those two was off the charts, since she and Ben had been the first to get together. Their honeymoon stage had to have worn off by now.

Nope. They both looked at each other across the room, a secret message passing between what could only be described as bedroom eyes.

I set the grocery bag down on the counter a little harder than necessary. I'd have to be careful opening the soda so it wouldn't spray everywhere, but the thump had gotten all the lovebirds' attention. "If sewing night has turned into couples night, then I'm out."

Not that I really wanted to sew or knew how, even after a year and a half of weekly get-togethers with that as the umbrella, but stewing in this pot of lovey-dovey nonsense had less appeal than inviting Tate back to the studio for a free recording session.

"Sorry, Bets." Jocelyn spun the jade beads on her wrist, looking chagrined.

I'd been surprised to see her when I'd rounded the hall, since she'd moved onto the Double B property up north to be closer to Malachi as she pursued her fashion career. Then I remembered that she and Malachi had driven down for the week so she could attend a symposium in the gaslight district in down-town San Diego.

"No more moon eyes." She crossed her heart.

"Speak for yourself." Drew lazily ran his thumb over Nicole's collar bone as he stared at her profile. But then he turned to me and winked.

Even I wasn't immune to his charms, though he didn't make me weak in the knees like melted plant-based butter as he did Nicole.

"Why don't you help me with these drinks, Drew?" He could open the ginger ale. A spray in the face with the carbonated sodas could help him cool off.

"Actually, I thought sewing night could literally be sewing night for a change." Molly sat up straight.

Amanda rubbed her knuckles, a worried pinch forming in the middle of her forehead. "I'm not sure I can." Her autoimmune disease often caused joint pain and swelling.

Peter held his paws—excuse me, *palms*—up in front of her. "I'll be your hands, darling."

I unscrewed the lid to the mason jars I'd brought along and poured some of the strawberry puree I'd made earlier into each of the glasses. The recipe for the mocktail was simple. Strawberry puree, ginger ale, sliced fresh strawberries, and ice. You could be fancy and add basil or mint, but I'd never been accused of being fancy a day in my life.

"How about I man the seam ripper and pick out any mistakes?" I asked as I stirred the final drink. I may not have used a sewing machine on any of the sewing nights, but I had gotten good at picking seams and cutting out patterns.

Molly looked at me over the bridge of her nose. A very teacherly scowl took over her face. She must have been practicing in a mirror, because it was better than her last attempt. Too bad I knew she was too sweet to ever be really intimidating. I stared back at her, crossing my arms over my chest for good measure. Her faux sternness couldn't compete with my Latina glare that had been handed down to me in my DNA.

Molly blinked and broke eye contact with a huff. "Please, Betsy. You're really the only one who doesn't know how. Well, besides Peter."

I flicked my gaze to Ben, then Drew. "What about Tweedle-Dee and Tweedle-Dum?"

"Doctors," Ben said matter-of-factly.

"We could sew pretty little stitches with our eyes closed," Drew added.

I handed Molly a glass of my strawberry mocktail that didn't have an official name but tasted delicious, then gave Jocelyn the glass in my other hand. "I don't really need to learn to sew though. My wardrobe consists of graphic tees and jeans." I ran a hand down my front, emphasizing my black V-neck with the words *A penny for your thoughts seems a little pricey*.

"For me?" Molly looked up at me with her big doe eyes.

Well, shoot. Her glare might not have been effective, but I couldn't say no when she looked at me like a puppy in the pound.

"Fine," I said on a sigh.

Jocelyn grinned and pulled out a stack of fabric from behind the sofa, spreading each bolt out onto the floor. "I have some more remnants out in Malachi's truck if no one likes these choices, but—" She looked up, her cheeks infusing with color in her excitement. "Nicole, I thought of you when I saw this." She held out a folded square of mustard yellow with tiny white flowers on it. "It's organic, fair trade, and sustainable."

Nicole reached to take the material, her eyes widening as soon as her hands caressed the top. "It's so soft."

Jocelyn pulled out another bolt, a solid wash of navy except for the band of burgundy at the bottom.

"The Condors' colors," Amanda squealed, beaming at Peter. Not only did she work as the football team's social media manager, but Peter played on the defensive line as well.

"The material is stretchy and breathable," Jocelyn pointed out.

Her hand paused on the next bolt as she looked between Drew and Ben. "I was going to select some fabric to make you guys some scrubs for work, but Malachi convinced me you'd appreciate team shirts for your hospital softball team instead. They're at the screen printers now and should be ready later this week."

"Thanks, man." Drew and Ben fist-bumped with Malachi who, as usual, had been content to sit back and enjoy the group silently from his spot beside Jocelyn. He spoke when necessary but hardly ever found words unavoidable.

"For you, Bets"—Jocelyn turned to me—"I found

this." A few yards of folded fabric were placed in my hand. Colorful miniature instruments in a winter palette—glacier blue tubas, coral keyboards, ice white trumpets, yellow guitars—blazed against a black back-drop. "I thought it would make a cute messenger bag for you to carry sheet music or whatever in."

"I might need a new bag when I go on tour," I murmured as I took the soft cotton blend.

"What!" Amanda shot forward on the couch, grimaced, but didn't settle back into Peter's inviting arm draped along the cushion. "You're going on tour? With who? Anyone famous? When do you leave? For how long? Where are you going? I have so many questions."

I met Amanda's Tigger-level enthusiasm with a measured regard. "I hadn't noticed."

She ignored my snark and leaned even farther forward, if that were possible. She was in jeopardy of falling off the couch as this point. "Tell me everything."

I shrugged like it was no big deal. Probably because it really wasn't. Not like Bono had approached me to do a world tour with him or anything. I hadn't even heard of True North until a few hours earlier, and they were a niche band that played worship music. No hate to worship music or anything. The songs were great to sing at church, and I knew a few singles had especially helped Amanda when she'd felt particularly overwhelmed or brought low because of her health.

"There's really not much to tell. In fact, I still need to call the guy and accept his offer."

Amanda waved her hands in the air. "Let me get this straight. You were asked to go on tour, which I'm assuming is like being drafted in the NFL, and you didn't immediately jump at the chance? Even if the singer you'd be working with is the equivalent of the 2008 Detroit Lions—they lost every single game, by the way—it's still a foot in the door, and you could be traded to another team, er, band or whatever."

Jocelyn cocked her head as she studied me. "Was it a musician who approached you or a manager?"

"Doesn't matter." *I'm not following where you're leading, Jocelyn.*

My friends looked at each other. "Musician," they chorused.

"Is it the spotlight thing? Is that why you have rules against getting close to artists even though you work with them every day?" Peter set down his empty glass. "I could give you some tips on how to deal with the media if that's the case."

No doubt his pointers would be more diplomatic than my *mind your own stupid business* would be. I smiled, though it probably looked more calculated than sweet on me. "Nosey paparazzi don't scare me."

"No, I imagine it would be the other way around," Ben said under his breath.

I flashed him another smile, this time showing teeth. If people were afraid of your bark, they'd stay far enough away that you didn't have to resort to a real bite.

"Why *do* you have a rule against dating musicians? I've always wondered." Amanda tapped the side of her chin with a nail.

"Why didn't you tell anyone about your health?" I quipped back. "We all have our reasons."

The second the words were out of my mouth, I realized they'd been the wrong thing to say. Instead of dropping the topic, eyes narrowed in focus. I might as well have thrown a bone to a pack of hungry dogs.

"You're hiding something." Molly's face fell. She'd taken Amanda's confession about keeping her health struggles a secret all this time much harder than the rest of us. Part of it was her need for everyone to be honest with her and each other, but a bigger part was her caring drive to mother everyone in sight.

"You dated a musician in the past and got your heart broken," Drew said with certainty.

I snorted. "Wrong."

His mouth pulled to the side. "You didn't date, but he strung you along and you got your heart broken."

I patted him on the knee. "Don't hurt yourself. My heart has never been broken by a musician or any other guy."

"There has to be some reason," he pressed. "People don't put walls around their hearts unless they're afraid of it getting hurt."

My gaze turned to steel as I locked eyes with Drew. "I am not afraid." I was smart. Big difference.

"Are you singing or working sound?"

The surprise of hearing Malachi ask the question caused me to blink and take a figurative step back.

"What? Why would you think I'd tour as a vocalist?"

He shrugged his western-shirt-clad shoulders. "My brother heard you, I guess. He says you're really good."

"No offense to your brother, but he doesn't always have the best judgement."

Malachi didn't say anything; just kept his gaze steady. It was...unnerving.

"My singing is reserved for the shower and in the car along with the radio. You will never see me on a stage."

"Never say never," Jocelyn singsonged.

"What's the guy's name?" Nicole asked.

"Who?"

"The one you're going on tour with." She held her phone in her hand. "I'm going to look him up."

Prickles of dread ran down my spine. Nicole googling him felt like they were forcing me to show my hand. Would they take one look at him and come to the same conclusion that I had? That Asher North, with his boyish lopsided grin, warm, intelligent eyes, and slightly longish curly hair was nothing more than a wolf in sheep's clothing waiting to catch me off guard so he could devour me in one bite? Or would they be taken in by his boy-next-door wholesomeness and the genuineness he seemed to project with a single glance?

Nicole watched me, her thumbs hovering over the phone screen as she waited for me to answer. I swallowed down my unease and notched my chin. The sharks would not circle without the scent of blood. If I projected an air of indifference, they'd believe it.

And maybe so would I.

"His name is Asher North, and he's the leader of the worship band called True North."

Nicole's head lowered as she focused on her search. "Oh." She glanced at me then back at her phone.

"What? Let me see." Amanda snatched the phone and studied the screen. "Wow." She tilted the screen to show Peter, who raised a single eyebrow. Soon the phone had been passed around the entire room.

Jocelyn cleared her throat. "I can see why you didn't immediately accept the job with him."

"You can?" Curiosity to know what they were all thinking ate at me, but years of practice kept my face bland.

"He makes you feel threatened." Nicole set her phone on the coffee table.

I pretended I didn't know what she meant. "If that were the case, I would've used my pepper spray on him."

"I'm kind of surprised she didn't," Ben whispered to Molly.

She swatted his shoulder and scrunched her nose at him.

"You guys are delusional." Mock derision could totally be used as a red herring. "Asher North is nothing more than your average egotistical narcissistic upstart musician. He didn't make, nor will he ever make, me feel any differently than any other person wanting to see their name on the top of the music charts."

"Slightly nauseous and disappointed with humanity?" Nicole asked.

I grinned. "Exactly."

4

Asher

*M*y muscles strained as I worked my way around the large buttress at the top of the pitch. My fingers had started to cramp two holds ago, protesting the amount of time it had been since I'd frequented my favorite climbing gym. This route, with its simulation of a range of climbing terrains from arêtes to overhangs, was one of the more difficult. As my thighs quivered with the exertion of pushing my body to the next grip in the progression, I reminded myself how much I enjoyed a good challenge.

"On belay?" someone from the ground below me asked their climbing partner.

"Belay on," came the reply.

I lifted my leg and inserted my toe into the tiny dimple carved out of the faux rockface, applying a small amount of pressure to make sure the grip was tight enough to hold my weight as I ascended.

"Climbing."

"Climb on."

I glanced down. My brother, Aaron, stared up at me, his jaw working as he chewed on a piece of Doublemint while holding my rope secure in case I slipped or lost my grip and fell.

"Tension or ready to lower?" he hollered up with a smirk.

Rock climbing translation: Do you need to rest by hanging on to the rope, or are you done climbing and want to return to the ground? Sibling translation: Are you so weak—both in body and mind—that you can't make it to the top and need to quit now in utter shame? Oh, and I'll rub it in your face for the foreseeable future if you do.

My fingers dug into the grip. "Climbing," I called down into his smug face.

He adjusted his hold on the rope, and I felt a small tug at the harness crossing my waist and upper thighs. "Climb on."

Sweat prickled my forehead. The last time I'd run this course I'd been able to climb to the top in about thirty minutes. I hadn't checked my wristwatch, but I wouldn't be surprised if twice that amount of time had lapsed.

The muscles in my arms and shoulders bulged as I gripped the edge of the summit. A bead of sweat trickled down my forehead and splashed onto my eyelashes, stinging my eye. I was half blinded as I pulled myself up onto the top of the wall with one eye closed like some kind of pirate. I just needed a cutlass between my teeth to make the picture complete. Instead, I lifted the hem of my shirt and mopped my face as I gulped in lungfuls of air-conditioned oxygen. Climbing could be a punishing mistress if you neglected her for too long.

My phone vibrated in my back pocket. I usually kept the device in my duffle bag when I climbed, but I must have forgotten to take it out of my pocket before strapping on my harness. Since I was at the gym, I didn't have a chalk bag or extra belays, ropes, or cara-biners to work around to dig my phone out, but I was still winded, so when I tapped to accept a call from an unfamiliar number, my hello came out all breathy.

"Umm...is this Asher North?" a female voice asked.

Seventh Street Sounds woman. I'd recognize her voice anywhere. I hadn't been able to get the quality of her tones out of my head since hearing her for the first time.

I tried to slow my breathing, but my lungs filled and emptied like they were bellows being worked by a brawny blacksmith. My heart knocking against the back of my ribs like a preschooler playing the xylo-phone for the first time didn't help things either.

I leaned over and rested my free hand on my knees. "This is Asher."

"I'm sorry to bother you so early in the morning. You sound like you're—"

There was a long, pointed pause.

"Oh. Oh!" Her words came fast and tight. "I am *so* sorry. I didn't think—" She cut herself off, but the sarcasm was thicker than a slice of Chicago deep dish pizza. "I didn't mean to interrupt who—I mean, what you were doing."

"What do you think I'm doing?" Sweat dribbled down my temple, and I wiped it away. Her insinuation hadn't exactly been made in a secret spy code that needed a cipher to be understood. I knew precisely what she didn't even bother to hint at. But considering how wildly presumptuous and judgmental her accusation, I thought it only fitting to make her squirm a bit. Maybe then she'd think twice before jumping to conclusions.

"Who or what you do is none of my business." Even with the sharp edge, her voice was still music. Too bad she wanted to cut me with her words.

"What's your name?"

"Excuse me?"

She seemed taken aback, and I couldn't stop the smile that spread across my face. "I have a right to know the name of my accuser, don't I?"

"I'm not—"

She stopped herself. Seemed she had a habit of doing that.

"Betsy Vargas. I'm the audio engineer you left your card with yesterday."

"Yes, I remember your voice." *It's imbedded itself into my brain.* Had taken over the majority of my thoughts. Had even done some interior decorating in there, so I doubted it would be going anywhere anytime soon. Which was fine by me. I had no plans to seek an eviction.

"This is a mistake," she said so quietly she must have been talking to herself.

She was going to hang up. I could feel it in all the squishy places most people tried to ignore or protect but that I went to when inspiration took hold of me.

"I'm rock climbing," I blurted out. "That's why I was out of breath when I answered. Not...well, not because of the reason you thought."

"Oh."

That was it. All she said. I waited in case more would come.

It didn't.

"Can I assume you're calling about the job?" Maybe I could guide the conversation in a better direction.

A tug on my harness pulled me forward to the edge of the wall. I leaned over and looked down. Aaron gestured big sweeping motions with his hands, his face a picture of spent patience. He may be at the end of my rope literally, but he was also at the end of his own metaphorically.

I held up a finger to let him know I'd be just

another minute. Now that I had Betsy on the phone, I couldn't let her hang up without some sort of commitment.

"How about we discuss it more over a cup of coffee in about an hour? At the roastery near your studio?" If I could sit down with her face-to-face, I knew I'd be able to convince her to sign on to the tour. Then I'd have more time to work on getting her on stage and sharing her voice with the world.

"Let me stop you right there, buddy."

Buddy? My smile widened.

"I don't date musicians. So whatever thoughts you have going on in your head, you can just nip them right in the butt."

"I think the saying is 'nip it in the bud,' not butt. Also, I don't have any thoughts in my head." Well, I had some. I wasn't dead, after all. "I take that back. I do have a thought. I think you should stop jumping to conclusions about me. The coffee suggestion was purely professional, I assure you. So we could talk over tour details and job specifics. That's all."

"Oh."

"And also, now, so you can apologize in person," I needled. I didn't actually need an apology. Seemed like whatever made her think the worst about me went deeper than our ten-minute interaction the day before. At least, I didn't think I'd said or done anything to make her automatically have a low opinion of me.

She made a noise which I deciphered as the word *fine* being pushed past clenched teeth.

"Excellent." I poured on cheer like salt on a wound to help the healing process. "See you in an hour."

As soon as I hung up, Aaron yanked on the rope, sending me careening toward the drop off. I scowled at him but yelled down, "On rappel."

Aaron made a *finally* gesture with his hand as he shouted, "Off rappel," and disengaged from the rope so I could abseil down.

"What took you so long?" Aaron slipped me a side-eye before clipping off the rope.

"Had to take a phone call at the top." I unhooked myself from the belay and stepped aside so another team of climbers could take my place and ascend the wall.

Aaron's elbow shot out and connected with my arm. He flashed me a cocky grin. "And what's your excuse for on the way up? I mean, I'm used to smoking you, but you usually give me a little more competition than that."

"Let's take it out to the real world, and we'll see who can be called king of the mountain." We lived in a mecca of amazing climbing spots from Joshua Tree only a couple of hours away to Yosemite, which made a great weekend getaway, and yet my brother only faced walls that were manmade for reasons I didn't understand. The gym was nice for a good workout and some training, but it nowhere near compared to the real deal.

Aaron shook his head. "Whatever, man." He checked his watch. "I need to hit the showers and head to work. Some of us have honest-to-goodness jobs to get to."

I unlatched the buckle of my harness and stepped out of the leg loops. "Don't hate because you have to punch a time clock and I don't."

"Since you're not hindered by *the man*, take care of this for me." He dumped his harness at my feet. "See ya later."

"I love you too," I called after his retreating back.

He kept walking but held up two fingers like the peace sign. An unspoken response between us to mean *love you too*.

After taking care of our equipment, I quickly showered and drove to the roastery where I'd told Betsy to meet me. The smell of coffee beans gave me a jolt as soon as I walked in the door—lightly caramelized and almost nutty. The three employees behind the counter moved in near choreography set to the rhythm of the grinder and the hiss emitting from the steam wand on the espresso machine. A low hum of voices as well as the clacking of a patron typing away on a laptop in the corner added to the symphony of a thriving business.

I scanned the dining room but didn't spot a woman whose stature belied the size of her personality. Small things were generally marked with the adjective *sweet*, but Betsy struck me as someone who'd shed that representation like an outgrown coat—if it'd ever fit her at all to begin with. I imagined Shakespeare had someone like her in mind when he wrote "Though she be but little, she is fierce." Then again, my high school English Lit class may've failed me, because I couldn't remember which character in which play had inspired that line. Oh well. The point remained. Betsy seemed like a handful that didn't appreciate any attempt at being handled.

The door opened behind me. I turned to step out of the way so I wouldn't block the person from joining the line to order but stopped at the revelation that the newcomer was none other than the woman I'd been waiting for. Her crown of tight spiral curls had been piled on top of her head and commanded to stay with nothing more than a flimsy elastic band. One whose authority was presently being questioned as an errant strand worked its way loose of its confines and sprang toward freedom to settle along the graceful curve of her exposed neck.

She had on a red-and-white-striped T-shirt and a pair of sunshine yellow headphones wrapped around the tops of her shoulders like a scarf. Her black-framed glasses only enlarged her caramel-colored eyes, which stared back at me with a half-challenging, half-guarded expression.

The glasses were new. I'd never been accused of being super observant—ninety-five percent of guys aren't, if we're honest—but as soon as I'd heard and then seen Betsy, it had been like she'd faded out all the sound and color around her and adjusted the dials on some invisible soundboard mixer to make herself come into complete focus.

It had happened before. When I'd been stuck on lyrics and inspiration struck in the most unusual of places. Or when I'd passed a man at a traffic light holding up a cardboard sign and I couldn't get him out of my mind. A supernatural poke and whispered command to pay attention.

"Stop staring at me like that." Betsy's mouth pressed into a thin line.

I blinked and looked away, embarrassed at being caught. "Like what?" Yes, okay, maybe I'd studied her longer than manners allowed, but it hadn't been *like* anything. I was supposed to pay attention, after all. How could I do that and not look at her?

"Like"—she waved her hand up and down the space in front of my body like a metal detector—"how you were."

I wanted to press and see if she'd straight-out accuse me of something this time. Instead, I took a step back. "I'm sorry if I made you uncomfortable."

She blinked, but not before I witnessed surprise flash across her eyes.

The customer in front of us moved down the counter. It was our turn to order. I looked to Betsy. Ladies first.

"I'll have a medium flat white."

I opened my mouth to add my order, my eyes on the menu.

"That will be all," Betsy said, her voice strict and brooking no argument.

I glanced down at her, and she met my gaze head on. Normally, I'd offer to pay for her drink. Because it was the gentlemanly thing to do and also because this was a work-related meeting and I wanted to hire her. All the vibes radiating from her small frame, however, told me to speak or reach for my wallet at my own risk.

Not a risk I was willing to take.

Once Betsy paid and I ordered my own cold foam cold brew, we found a free table off to the side. She sat, spine rigid. She appeared more sentry on duty than potential employee.

"How's your morning been so far?" Pleasantries were always a good place to start. Maybe they'd help her relax a bit. Let her know that I was completely harmless—and really, why wasn't that her initial starting place to begin with?

She regarded me warily, her shoulders relaxing not an inch. "So far so good."

I leaned back in my chair, projecting nonchalance and openness. "I'm glad to hear it."

The barista called our names and set down two cups on the counter. Betsy made to stand, but I beat her to it.

"I'll grab them."

She seemed to deliberate, then lowered herself back to the seat.

It only took a few seconds to retrieve our drinks and return to the table. Betsy accepted her hot coffee and blew across the small hole in the lid before taking a tentative sip.

She set the coffee cup down. Her fingers fiddled with the cardboard sleeve wrapped around the cup.

Was that a hint of vulnerability to her movements?

She looked up. Her eyes glinted.

Okay, maybe not.

"Was the price you are willing to pay that you wrote on the back of your card real, or are you screwing with me and wasting my time?"

I wiped the top of my lip in case the cold foam had left a white Gomez Adams pencil mustache there. "I assure you, I'm not"—I couldn't say *screwing*. Maybe it was prudish of me, but I couldn't help but picture my granny clutching her pearls at what she'd deem vulgar language—"*messing* with you. True North is in desperate need of a skilled sound engineer, and we're coming down to the wire to procure one."

She took another sip of her coffee. "When does the tour start?"

"In a little less than two weeks."

"Where will you be playing?"

"Fairly local. Just the southwest. A few spots within the southern counties of California along with some venues in Arizona and Nevada."

"Duration?"

"Four weeks."

She paused, seeming to think. "I have some stipula-
tions. Two, to be precise."

I nodded. Not out of the ordinary if she wanted to
call shotgun because she got car sick or insisted on
working with her own equipment even though we'd
recently purchased some specifically for touring. "I'm
sure we can be accommodating."

Her shoulders pressed back even farther. "The first
thing is that no one in the band can develop any sort of
romantic feelings for me or ask me out."

I waited for her to crack a smile, laugh, and say she
was only teasing.

She met my gaze in an unblinking stare.

"Like in *A Walk to Remember*? 'You have to promise
not to fall in love with me.'" I tried to impersonate
Mandy Moore as Jamie Sullivan but failed miserably.

Betsy's brows dipped. "What?"

I took a nice draw from my cold brew. "It's a movie
based off a Nicolas Sparks book. Tell me you've
seen it."

She pulled her cup closer. "Sorry."

"Okay. No problem. We'll add it to our movie list
for the bus. I'll be sure to pack extra tissues, because it's
a tear-jerker."

"Umm…" For the first time, Betsy's spine touched
the back of her chair. She looked as though a street
hustler had played the shell game with her and she was

trying to figure out how the pea wasn't under the shell she'd thought it was under.

Guess my response had thrown her. "I'm sorry to say I can't tell you that it's not a problem." I was doing an awful job of suppressing my grin.

Her eyes were unfocused in her confused state. "Huh?"

"To your first stipulation. In the movie, Landon tells Jamie that it's not a problem after she makes him promise he won't fall in love with her. Want to wager a guess what ends up happening?"

Her lips pushed to the side. "He falls in love with her."

I made a finger-pistol motion with my hand. "Bingo. So I can't make you any such promises, because then we know what the inevitable outcome would be, don't we?"

If I didn't know any better, I would have sworn Betsy made a little groan-growl sound from her side of the table. But it was probably just the noise of the busy café around us.

"What's stipulation number two?" I asked. We were so close to the finish line on getting her on board.

She took a deep breath, her fingers back on the cardboard sleeve, spinning it around the edge of her cup. "I was wondering if…"

If I could perform with you.

If I could have my own solo.

If you'd write a song for me.

Yes, yes, and yes.

"If I could have part of the fee up front."

She was the wave toppling my castles made of sand. I redirected my thoughts away from dreams to business. "Of course. How does three equal payments sound? One third now, a third halfway through, and a third once the tour is complete."

"That would be good, thank you." Her shoulders finally loosened, if only by a fraction.

I held out my hand for her to shake and make it official. "Welcome to True North, Betsy."

"Thank you." She pumped my hand twice, then let go. "Oh, there was one more thing. I just wanted to make sure you understood I'm only signing on to be your audio person. I'm strictly behind the scenes. No singing."

Now *that* I hadn't shaken an agreement on.

I felt a little like Santa must on Christmas morning. Except I'm real and there was no way I was going to ding-dong-ditch this good news. I wanted to see the looks on everyone's faces when I told them I had the money to start the process of getting Camilla a green card.

I glanced at the clock on my dashboard. If I hurried, I'd be able to catch all the adults at the same time. There was a twenty-minute overlap when Papi got home from the night shift at the newspaper before Mami and Tia Alma left to whichever client's house they were cleaning that day and Tio Sergio took the little ones to school before continuing his job search.

Our small craftsman was bursting at the seams, but I knew Mami especially liked having her sister close. Once Tio Sergio found steady employment, they'd start looking for a house for themselves, although I doubted they'd move too far away. Then again, housing in Southern California wasn't easy to come by, and a person needed to build a time machine and pluck some gold nuggets out of the river like a regular forty-niner to be able to afford four walls and a roof.

On a street full of houses with stucco façade and tile roofs, ours was the only dwelling with cedar shingle siding. It stuck out like it didn't belong, and yet I liked this house more than any of the others. Maybe there was a deeper meaning there. Maybe I just didn't like Spanish-style architecture. Could go either way.

I parked and hurried along the concrete walkway toward the front door. Asher had used an app to transfer the money from the band's bank account to my own. All I had to do was write Papi or Tio a check. The family hadn't decided which option would be best in getting Camilla to the States so she could stay permanently. Fly her over on a B visa and hope the process of obtaining a green card could be expedited within the one-hundred-and-eighty-day window, or save the money the plane ticket would cost and allow my father to be the sponsor, since he'd become a citizen over a decade before. Citizen sponsors bumped the preference to first from second with a permanent resident sponsor.

But then it could take who-knew-how-long until my cousin was reunited with her family. Yes, she was twenty-one and officially an adult, but those in the United States didn't fully understand the family relationship dynamics of people in Latin American countries. Leaving Camilla in Argentina had to have been like leaving half of her heart for my aunt. And even though Camilla had tried to sound positive last time I talked with her, there had been a hollowness to her words. Logically, she knew her parents and siblings had to take the opportunity when it presented itself, but deep down she felt a little abandoned. How could she not? She didn't have a single member of her family left in the country.

At least she's safe, I told myself. Unlike a lot of others seeking to make a new life in the United States, my cousin's safety wasn't being threatened. There wasn't a desperation, a life-or-death outcome dependent on her being here now. We had the time to wait and go through the proper channels. To do things the legal way with paperwork, red tape, and sometimes years of waiting. Not everyone had that luxury.

"Hola!" I called loud enough so I could be heard throughout the house. "I have good news!"

Mami poked her head out of the downstairs bathroom doorway, a tube of lipstick in her hand. "Ah, *mija*, no need to shout."

Stampeding elephants herded down the stairs in the form of Diego and Ava. "Betsy, can we have a dance party before school?" Ava asked.

"*Por favor.*" Diego looked up with pleading eyes.

I patted them both on the head. "Maybe after I talk with the grown-ups. Here." I pulled out my phone and opened the music app, finding the sound track for *Encanto,* then starting "We Don't Talk About Bruno." Lin-Manuel Miranda was a genius. "Practice your moves, then when I'm done, you can show me what you've got."

Diego snatched my phone out of my hand while Ava sashayed after him.

"Now, what is this hollering about good news?" Papi lowered himself into a chair, his head heavy on his neck like he could barely keep it upright any longer. If he didn't make it upstairs soon, his chin would hit his chest and he'd snore right here for the next six hours.

"Where are Tio Sergio and Tia Alma?" I looked around but didn't see either of them.

"*Hermanos!*" Papi's voice boomed.

Tia Alma descended the stairs, her hands by her ear as she secured the back of an earring to its post. Tio Sergio was right behind her. She made a sucking noise with her teeth. "The neighbors will complain if you keep shouting."

Papi made a rolling motion with his hand in my direction. "Betsy has something to say."

Four pairs of eyes stared at me. "I have the money for Camilla."

Tia Alma inhaled a sharp breath and covered her mouth with steepled palms.

"Well, maybe not all, but I have enough to start at least."

Mami pulled me to her side and kissed my temple. "*Cómo?*"

Of course she would ask how, seeing as I usually only brought in enough income to make rent on the studio and pay for my room and board here. Maybe it sounded weird that I still lived at home, but we were South American. Living with our parents until we married was a part of our cultural heritage. Mami would probably have a heart attack if I moved out before I had a ring on my finger.

"I was hired as a live sound engineer for a band going on tour. They paid me part of the fee up front."

"I am speechless." Tio Sergio enveloped me in a bear hug. "*Gracias, sobrina*. We will repay you when we can."

I shooed away his comment. "Nonsense. Family helps family, no?"

Papi's eyes beamed with pride. "Sí."

"So," Mami interrupted. "Who is this band?"

Worry clouded my mother's expression. With good reason. She didn't trust musicians any more than I did.

We hadn't always been this way. Although, if we had, could anyone really blame us? Musicians' reputations were notorious. They wrecked hotel rooms, misused illegal substances, and slept with groupies without even bothering to get a name first. And that was just what the media reported. Who knew what kind of other activities they participated in when people weren't looking? But despite all that, we'd put aside our misgivings and given a musical artist a chance once. All he'd done in return was broken hearts, shattered lives, and solidified our mistrust against all like him.

I took my mother's fingers in my hands. "Don't worry, Mami. I won't do anything stupid."

She tilted my head down to kiss my forehead. "I know you won't, mija." She lifted my chin and looked into my eyes. "But I am your mother, and I will always worry about you because I love you."

The instrumental version of "Dos Oruguitas" filled the living room as my cousins scampered in.

"Are we done talking yet?" Diego asked.

"Yeah. You are taking *forever*." Ava and her theatrics.

I tweaked her nose and took my phone back from Diego, pressing play on a song in a different playlist. Striking a pose, I grinned down at my cousins. "Because we are Argentine"—I thickened my accent to comical levels—"we tango."

Diego and Ava giggled. I pulled Diego close to me while Tio did the same with Ava. As the music played, we adopted exaggerated steps. High kicks, slow shuffles, and arms extended out like arrows in front of us as we prowled from one end of the room to the other.

"No, no, no, no." Papi stood, wiping his palms against the air like he could erase what he'd just witnessed. "You are a disgrace to your heritage. I disown you all." He winked before adopting a smolder Flynn Ryder would be jealous of and aiming it at Mami (Seriously, if Disney wanted a leading man with a *real* smolder, they should have made him Latino.) He held out a hand to Mami. "Should we show them how it's done, *mi vida?*"

Mami blushed as she slipped her palm against Papi's. With a tug, he pulled her to his chest and slid his other hand to rest on the small of her back. Their eyes locked, and the dance began. No matter where their feet took them or what steps they mastered, they never took their eyes off each other the entire time.

The front door opened, and I turned to see my baby sister with her own baby on her hip.

I wished I could've said the guilt of the sight had worn off, but that would've been a lie. Guilt always came, followed quickly by anger.

"A dance party without me?" Bella let the diaper bag fall from her shoulder to the ground with a thud. She moved baby Charlotte from her hip to her front and held her daughter's tiny arm out to the side as she swayed left to right.

Bella smiled, but the happy expression did nothing to mask the strain around her mouth or the tired bags under her eyes. Bella should've been missing sleep to study for final exams, not because an infant kept her up all night.

Resolve hardened in my gut. Asher North could flash his charming smile and study me as if he could see past my thick outer layer of sarcasm all he wanted.

I would not be moved.

6

Asher

Noise
All around me
Seeping into me
Drowning out your voice

I tapped the eraser end of my pencil onto my notebook as I read the lines for the sixth time. What came next? Unfortunately, that noise on the page had ratcheted up in volume between my ears.

I sighed and tossed my pencil on top of the paper. My head needed to clear before anything else would come to me. I picked out a simple tune on the strings. One that took zero concentration and mental acuity but allowed my mind to follow the pattern.

We needed a few more songs to add to our playlist. I'd been hoping to get at least five written to share with the rest of the band and get their opinion on which we should debut to a live audience on the road.

But to do that, we'd need time to practice the songs. And to practice the songs, I had to actually write them.

I could hear snippets. A simple melody here. A small stanza there. But so far, nothing had come together like I wanted it to. Like I needed it to.

I closed my eyes and picked out the melody that had played on a loop along the edges of my consciousness. The key of D. With my pinky resting at the pickguard, I used my other four fingers to pluck at the strings over the sound hole. My heartbeat slowed. Played percussion to the tune. Kept rhythm. When it felt right, I added my voice to the mix, singing the small sample of lyrics that I'd read so many times I'd already memorized them.

Noise
All around me
Seeping into me
Drowning out your voice

I played through the tune again, more words slowly forming in my mind's eye. I didn't stop to write them down. Instead, I let the music come together like an artist blending colors to try and create the perfect hue.

Just a whisper
Let me hear you
Let me feel you
Above all the noise

Hmm. Maybe it would sit more comfortably in a different key. I picked up my capo and clipped the device to the guitar's fingerboard to shorten the strings and raise their pitch.

Speak to me
E – F – G
You're all I need.
F – G – A – B flat
Drown out the world
A – A – B flat – A
Lord, I'm listening
G – F – C – C

The doors to the sanctuary burst open, cutting off the flow of inspiration like a clamp to a blood vessel.

"Well, those were lighter than I thought." Betsy turned to glare at the swinging double doors behind her. When she faced forward again, she grimaced. "Sorry. I didn't mean to interrupt. I was hoping to sneak in and check out the equipment without disturbing you, but that's obviously an epic fail."

"It's okay." I set my guitar down beside me on the stage. "Just let me jot down those lyrics, and I'll show you around."

She walked down the aisle and stopped near the second row of seats.

Ah. How did that first line of the second stanza start again? I hummed out the tune, mentally singing the first bit. I hit a blank wall.

"Something about a whisper," I mumbled to myself, willing the words to come back to me.

"Just a whisper. Let me hear you. Let me feel you—"

Betsy sang so quietly I was surprised her voice traveled to me at all.

I looked up at her and sang along with the line. "Above the noise."

Her mouth softened, and I thought she'd smile, but then her lips pressed into a thin line, and she looked away. Quickly, I jotted the lyrics in my notebook before I forgot them again, then stood up and stretched out my back. Hunching over a notebook and guitar while sitting on the top step of the stage did nothing for my posture.

"Thank you," I said, meaning it. That part of the song could have been lost to me forever if she hadn't remembered what she'd heard.

She shoved her hands into the pockets of her jeans and rocked on the balls of her feet, refusing to acknowledge my gratitude. Her gaze bounced around the large worship space, setting upon anything but me.

Was she...afraid of me?

As soon as the idea took shape, Betsy whipped her head around and pinned me with narrowed eyes rife with challenge. Almost as if she dared me to say my question out loud.

I swallowed hard, pushing down equal parts intimidation and intrigue.

Betsy did intimidate me. Although, maybe not in the way she meant to. The number of times I caught myself thinking of her was a bit frightening. But in a thrilling sort of way. All of her hard edges that she'd sharpened to keep people out made me even more interested in finding the soft center she tried so hard to protect.

"The equipment," she said tersely.

"Over here." I led her to our soundboard, set up to the side of the stage. One of the PA guys from the church had come to unbox the equipment and plug in all the mics, amplifiers, and keyboard, but so far, we hadn't practiced with anything turned on. We'd been waiting for our engineer. For Betsy.

She ran her hand over the plethora of nobs and switches, a small smile dancing at the corners of her lips. An invisible band around my chest loosened. This was True North's first tour. I wanted it to be a success, which was why I'd spent a small fortune on the new sound system. An investment in our future. Betsy's facial expression hadn't changed much, but there was approval in the subtle markers. I'd take it.

The side door to the sanctuary opened, and the rest of the band filed in, Tricia bringing up the rear with a waddle any penguin would be proud of. I clapped my hands together but stopped shy of rubbing my palms against each other like a villain with an evil plan that was all coming together. I did have a plan and it looked as if it would work out, but there wasn't anything nefarious about it.

I peeked at Betsy out of the corner of my eye. At least, *I* didn't think my plan devious. Others could come to their own conclusions.

"Guys," I called to get the newcomers' attention. "We have a new member of the team. I'd like you all to meet Betsy Vargas."

Jimmy stepped forward and shook Betsy's hand. "I'm Jimmy. I play the keyboard, and this is my son Marcus, who plays bass."

Betsy dipped her head to them both.

"That's Dave at the drums," I said.

Dave saluted the room with a stick to his brow.

"And Tricia is our female vocal."

"Nice to meet you." Tricia smiled warmly.

"You want to tell the group a little about yourself, Betsy? Help us get to know you better?" I knew she didn't. I'd only interacted with her a couple of times, but that was all it had taken to read her like a book— though she thought she kept her covers closed tighter than a censorship zealot banning literature.

Sure enough, her jaw tightened as she worked to bite back a quick retort. "Kumbaya moments aren't really my thing."

I grinned at her, my smile widening at the surprise that flashed across her face at my response. She'd probably thought I would be offended or upset. Nothing could've been farther from the truth. "See? We're already learning so much about you."

She ignored me and shimmied out of a lightweight flannel overshirt.

Tricia snickered. "I love your tee."

Betsy pulled at the hem of her shirt as she looked

down. I followed her line of sight. Across her chest it read *I can't be held responsible for what my face does when you talk*. I held back a burst of laughter.

Betsy lifted her head, a smug bow to her mouth. "No one can say they haven't been warned."

"How very, uh, kind of you?" Jimmy scratched at his temple as he shared a slightly scared look with his son.

"Now that we're all besties, can we get started, or are we going to sit around and braid each other's hair first?" Betsy's hands found her curvaceous hips as she stood off in front of me.

I reached up and fingered one of my short curls. "*Could* you braid my hair?"

She rolled her eyes, the motion making me unexplainably happy. Betsy's eye rolls could be turned into a drinking game—never mind the little detail that I didn't drink.

She breezed past me to the cables that ran along the floor and hooked up to the inputs on the soundbar. "I'm going to get everything in order. Give me a few minutes."

She worked with efficiency, the grace of someone who knew her business. Once everything was in place, she smiled. A real smile. A hit-you-with-an-anvil-to-the-chest-Wile E. Coyote-style kind of smile.

"I think we're ready. Asher, I need you to check your mic for me."

I jumped over the steps and straight onto the stage

and took my spot behind the central microphone. "Testing, one, two."

Betsy shook her head. "I need you to sing something. 'I'm a Little Teapot' should do."

I stared at her.

She stared right back.

"Fine." I capitulated even though I wasn't sure why I couldn't start in on one of our own songs. Wouldn't she need to know the compression and EQ of those? Instead, I did as she said and sang the famous children's ditty.

She stopped me at *handle*. "I need you to do the motions."

I studied her face, looking for a hint that she was laying one over on me. A twitch of her cheek. A crinkling of her eyes.

She looked back at me as steady as could be.

"Why?"

"Because"—she spoke slowly as if to a child—"no one stands completely still behind their mic when they're performing. I need to hear how the mic picks up when you're moving around."

Okay, that actually made sense. Maybe she wasn't having a laugh at my expense. I started the song over, creating a handle by placing one hand on my waist and a spout by arching the other in a downward angle. I tipped when the song said to, to the accompaniment of strangled chuckles from the guys behind me.

"Will you sing that to the baby when she's born?" Tricia asked around her laughter.

Betsy's face nearly glowed when I turned to her. "Got what you needed?"

Her palms rested on the soundboard as she leaned forward and locked her gaze with mine. "I got *exactly* what I wanted."

7

Betsy

"*I* think that's a wrap for today." Asher pulled his bright-orange guitar strap over his head, then placed the instrument in its case. "Good work today, everyone."

Tricia gave a thumbs-up as she guzzled water from a bottle. I eyed her baby bump. Either the woman was baking more than one tiny human in there or she was nearing her due date.

Reason number two-hundred-thirty-three why musicians were idiots: they thought going on tour when one of their lead vocalists was ready to pop was a good idea. Talk about selfish narcissism. Tricia probably didn't think she had a choice. Either she went and performed like a well-trained circus monkey, or she lost her place and all she'd been working for.

Tours were no joke. Long days on the road. Hours on your feet in front of unforgiving audiences. Terribly unhealthy food from drive-throughs. Sleepless nights on hard beds in cramped spaces.

I wanted to march right up to Asher and rip his Christian mask off his too-handsome face, then flick him right between the eyeballs. He could sing about God's love until he was blue in the face, but I didn't believe his sincerity for a second when he put his own ambitions for fame and fortune above his supposed friend's health and that of her unborn child.

"Mamacita's Cantina?" Asher looked up from fastening his guitar case shut, unaware of my seething and my wish to cause him physical harm.

Tricia wiped water from her chin. "I could totally go for one of their smothered burritos right about now."

Jimmy unplugged Marcus's bass from the amplifier. "What's your homework situation looking like?" he asked his son.

Marcus winced. "Biology test in the morning."

"I'll help you study." Jimmy turned to Asher. "We'll have to take a raincheck on dinner. Maybe next time."

I'd learned earlier that Marcus attended the local public high school instead of homeschooling. They had worked it out with his teachers so that he could go on this tour with True North, although I really didn't see how he was going to be able to juggle a full school workload with the rigors of tour life. Hopefully he didn't get car sick, since his future held a lot of hours reading on a moving vehicle, and I didn't really want to smell vomit while driving across the desert.

Asher gave Jimmy a two-finger salute. "Tell Doreen I said hi."

"Will do." He gathered his stuff, and the two walked out the side door.

Here's my chance. I could follow in the father/son Beeman shadow and slip out before anyone noticed. Not that I was a coward. I just didn't want to get fired for throat-punching my boss on the first day.

I'd only taken a couple of steps when Asher pinned me with a razor-sharp look. "Betsy."

My shoulders squared as I faced him. I didn't care what he said; he'd hired me to do a job, and my duties for the day were over. He wasn't entitled to any more of my time. Even if Mexican food sounded delicious and my stomach chose that moment to growl. I wasn't willing to endure the side helping of heartburn sharing a meal with someone so egocentric would bring. Because despite how *nice*—why did that sound like a different four-letter word in my brain?—Asher had presented himself to be so far, I knew it was an act. Forcing Tricia on a tour in her third trimester proved it.

"Oh, yes, please come." Tricia looked at me, hopeful. "I'm always surrounded by guys. Rescue me."

She laughed at her joke, but I froze where I stood. Asher I could have ignored. Told off even. But Tricia was another story. If I walked away, I'd be no better than the other self-absorbed males in the band. No better than *him*.

I pasted on a smile, then reapplied glue when the upward slant of my lips didn't stick. "How could I say no to that?"

"I'll meet you guys there." Dave stuck his drumsticks in his back pocket and exited stage left.

Asher had assured me earlier that the church was fine with us leaving all the equipment up throughout the week, so I didn't bother unplugging anything or coiling the long lengths of cables running along the blue carpet. I'd get enough of a workout over the next couple of months lugging the coils of cables around. My arms would be nice and trim.

Asher descended the stage with his guitar case in his hand. "You can follow me to the restaurant."

Tricia waddled past me up the aisle, so I waited a moment to give her a head start so I didn't feel like I was in a traffic jam on I-5 stuck behind a grandma driver. I hated driving slow, but I hated walking slow even more, and passing Tricia as she panted up the slight incline seemed incredibly rude and heartless.

Asher pulled up behind me, his palm out like he planned to place it along the small of my back to help steer me up the aisle. "Shall we?"

He was essentially a tail-riding sports car inching closer from the middle lane. He could pass me, but he wouldn't. I had two choices: tap my brakes and risk a fender-bender, or speed off before contact was made.

No matter how much I wanted to dig in my heels and stand rooted where I was—stand for all women against all men who pushed them places they didn't want to go —I lengthened my stride and sped up the aisle before his fingers could find contact with my skin.

Outside, Tricia finger waved at me as I passed her car to unlock my clunker, then she pulled away. Thankfully, the engine cranked right up instead of coughing and spluttering like a chain smoker that inhaled two cartons of cigarettes a day. The sentence *Will you give me a jump?* would never pass my lips, even in referring to my car's battery.

Mamacita's Cantina ended up being only a few minutes' drive from the church. Arched entryways and windows had been cut out of the stuccoed exterior, the trim painted a vibrant red and the green roof making the building patriotic as it sported the colors of the Mexican flag. Soft Mariachi music played in the background, but it was the smell of fresh tortillas and cilantro that really welcomed guests as soon as they walked in the front door.

The hostess seated us right away—a table not too far from the entrance. Tricia squatted over the seat beside mine, her palms planted on the table as she lowered herself into the chair.

Yeah, a very pregnant lady on a concert tour was a super good idea.

Dave picked up his menu with one hand, his index finger tapping along the edge. I followed his example even though I already knew what I'd order. In contrast to Nicole's vegan sensibilities, I was very much connected to my Argentine culture when it came to food—namely, I could eat a Texan under the table when it came to beef. Malachi's family cattle ranch was safe as long as I and those like me lived by the slogan *Beef, it's what's for dinner.*

A server stopped at our table with a tray of waters. She set an ice-cold dimpled red cup down in front of each of us. Her black hair was pulled back into a pony-tail, but a strand around her face had come loose and stuck to the corner of her mouth. "Can I take your order, or do you need a couple more minutes?" she asked in accented English.

Eyebrows rose in silent inquiry as we all looked at each other around the table. "I think we're ready." Asher smiled at the server, then looked to Tricia. "Ladies first."

Tricia ordered the smothered burrito she had mentioned back at the church. The server moved her gaze to me after she'd finished writing.

"Yo quiero la orden de tacos de carne asada, con tortillas de maíz y extra limón. Gracias."

"Algo de beber?" she asked as she jotted down my order of thin steak tacos and corn tortillas with extra lemons.

"La horchata, es receta original o es hecha en una máquina?"

"Sí, es hecha aquí y sabe muy bien. El dueño hace la receta de su bisabuela."

"Entonces me da una, por favor." The sweetened rice milk spiced with cinnamon was one of my favorite drinks as long as the restaurant made it fresh and it wasn't on tap like soda from a machine.

Dave and Asher ordered, but as soon as the server left, I found three pairs of eyes staring at me.

"What?" I pulled my water cup closer and took a sip.

"You speak Spanish like a native."

I cut Dave a withering glower. I hated when people made assumptions based off skin tone. My friend Juan couldn't speak a lick of Spanish even though he was as brown as toffee. But Hispanics and whites alike assumed he knew the language because of that alone. And I, well, my skin reflected the history of European migration and influence in Argentina. None of our neighbors automatically assumed or even suspected we were an immigrant family, because we *passed*. We passed as born in the good ole U-S-of-A because we didn't *look* how people assumed all Hispanics and immigrants from Central and South America looked. Our story and experience with racism within these borders wasn't the same as many other immigrant families because of our light skin inherited from our European bloodlines, and that made me angry. And sad. And, quite frankly, also inspired a guilt-inducing amount of relief.

"Maybe that's because I'm Latina." I kept my voice monotone, a silent *duh* punctuating my sentence.

"But—" Dave looked like he had two puzzle pieces in his hands that he swore fitted together, but no matter how hard he forced them, they just wouldn't line up right.

I rolled my eyes. Nothing added after that *but* would be good. Better to cut him off and steal his shovel before he dug himself deeper into a pit of ignorance supported by splintered beams of good intentions.

"My parents immigrated from Argentina when I wasn't much older than a baby." I splayed my fingers across the lacquered table top, hoping that small morsel would give them all something to chew on for a while. At least until our food came.

"Oh." Tricia's eyes rounded as she pressed a hand to the side of her belly. "Speaking of babies, want to feel mine kick? She's going to be a soccer player for sure."

"I really don't—"

Oh, okay. I'm touching another woman's stomach.

Tricia had her fingers wrapped around my wrist, forcing my hand against her taut skin. Seriously, her skin felt like a rubber band ready to snap. Had to be super uncomfortable for her.

Kind of like I felt at this exact moment. A light tugging of my arm proved her grip solid. I wouldn't get my hand back without hurting her feelings. Time to let a fetus use my palm as a soccer ball.

A hard shove against my fingers had Tricia squealing. "Did you feel that?"

She finally let go of my wrist, and I pulled my hand out of her reach.

"She'll grow up to give Lionel Messi's record a run for its money."

My heart twisted, memories flooding over me and making me feel like a piece of threadbare cotton being raked over an old-timey washboard. I couldn't help but compare Tricia's excitement and exuberance at the life inside her with my sister's depression when she'd been pregnant. She was better now; we were all thankful. The birth of my niece, Charlotte, had seemed to lift her out of her despair, but there had been months there when we'd all held our breath. When we weren't vocally calling down curses on a certain poor excuse for a human, that is. But Bella should've had this joy that radiated from Tricia's countenance. She'd been robbed.

And it was all my fault.

"You guys should be ashamed of yourselves."

Dave and Asher sat across the table from me, but I pictured a third person there. Someone who deserved more than just a tongue lashing. I shook my head, trying to dislodge him from my mind. There were similarities, sure—musicians and a woman on the cusp of motherhood—but I had to remind myself the situations were also different. Otherwise, I might lunge across the table and—

It didn't matter. There would be no lunging.

Dave's and Asher's eyes widened.

"Making Tricia travel and perform in her condition is completely selfish."

"Woah. Hold on now." Asher raised his hands, palms out. I'd seen Malachi make the same gesture to a startled horse he'd tried to calm down.

Do you think I'm not calm, Asher? I assure you, you don't want to see not calm.

"I think there's been a misunderstanding."

I crossed my arms over my chest. I understood everything perfectly.

Tricia touched my shoulder. "They aren't making me go on tour, Betsy." She laughed a little. "In fact, they've all been trying to talk me out of it for months."

Say what now? My arms fell at my side.

Tricia's cheeks pinkened. "It's sweet that you got so protective of me."

Asher cocked his head. The way he studied me made it seem like he'd put on some type of x-ray vision glasses. He was peeling back the layers. Sweet? Sure, but he suspected more.

I squirmed in my seat. Where was the server with our food?

"The truth is," Tricia continued, "I need the distraction. My husband is deployed and may not be back by the time the baby is born. I don't want to sit at home worried about him or about having to bring this baby into the world by myself."

"You're not alone, Trish." Asher smiled at her the way a brother would. "We're your family away from family."

Tricia dabbed at her eyes with a napkin and returned his smile with a watery one of her own.

The server approached with a tray of steaming and sizzling food. As she set down the first plate, she said, "Careful. It's hot."

Our meal wasn't the only thing giving off heat. Chagrin burned in my gut. Was it possible that I had misjudged Asher? And if so, what exactly did that mean?

8

Asher

$\mathcal{P}$rofessional music as a ministry was not unlike tightrope walking. On the one hand, you needed to garner enough of a presence that your ministry reached as many people as it could so more hearts would be impacted. On the other hand, the more your name was recognized, the greater the risk of falling off that super skinny rope. And boy was it a long way down. You could trip on forgetting the reason you sang in the first place and who you sang for, blinded by the limelight. Or a strong wind of discord could blow you off, people challenging your very heart and character as a Christian.

I had no intention of getting a big head and becoming unbalanced as I walked the line. And as long as my mother was my mother, I didn't need to worry about that happening. If my ego ever inflated just a little, she'd take a pin to it and pop that thing in under a tenth of a second.

"Have you decided to grow up and get a real job yet?" Cynthia North only considered careers that required college degrees, set business hours, provided 401Ks, and had bosses breathing down your neck as "real jobs." My profession, of course, didn't tick off any of those boxes, so I was wasting my life, according to her.

Her salon-styled sleek bob shone under the chandelier hanging above the massive dining room table. Enough chairs skirted the perimeter of the gilded-edge oak slab to house a dinner party, but only the three of us —Mother, Aaron, and I—sat around the ensemble. One would think we'd be congregated as a cozy trio at the end of the table. One would be wrong. We sat sparsely, evenly separated and spaced. We wouldn't have even been able to pass each other dishes of food had the courses actually been placed in front of us. Instead, a long arrangement of out-of-season begonias and lighted candles ran central to the wood grain while Mother's professional chef dished up culinary snobbery in the kitchen and presented each of our plates to us on golden chargers.

"Why can't you be more like your brother?" Mother sniffed as she dabbed the corner of her mouth with a cloth napkin.

Aaron set his fork beside his plate. If we'd been anywhere other than at Mother's, he would have plunked his elbow on the table and rested his chin in his hand. But we'd had the backs of our heads slapped enough as kids to know better than to ever display such base manners in front of Cynthia North.

"Yeah, Asher. You should be more like me." He grinned wickedly.

If the table hadn't been big enough to save Rose, Jack, and the rest of the cast of *Titanic* from a freezing, watery grave, I would've kicked him in the shin.

Mother, of course, didn't pick up on his teasing tone. In her eyes, Aaron could do no wrong. Despite the odds stacked against us, what with her devotion toward him and apathy toward me, my brother and I had a pretty decent relationship. Did I wish Mother would recognize that I wasn't a deadbeat simply because my career didn't follow her rubric of success? Sure. What son didn't want his mother's approval? In fact, I had to stop myself every once in a while and examine my motivations. Were my actions based on my mother's voice in my head, or were they truly the right thing to do?

Take Betsy for example. I really wanted to get her singing in front of an audience with the band. Why? Was it because a new voice and sound like hers could catapult us to a larger platform that might actually garner a positive reaction from people in general and my mom specifically? Or was it because I knew deep down she had something to share, something the world needed to hear, and she was just the person to spread that unique message?

Honestly? I was pretty sure my motivation stemmed from the latter reason, but there was a part of me that feared a little of the first was mixed in as well.

Mother sighed dramatically. "If your father were still alive, he'd know what to do to make you see reason. He'd stop your tomfoolery."

I picked up my water glass and took a drink. When she got like this, the best course of action was no action at all. If I didn't respond, then she'd lose steam and move on. Sometimes to another subject she thought I wasn't doing right. Like—

"Have you started seeing anyone, at least, Asher?" The skin above her top lip wrinkled as she puckered her mouth. "Although, women like men who can provide for them, and you'd need a real job for that."

I looked across the table at Aaron and locked eyes with him. He imperceptibly shook his head.

My turn to grin at his discomfort. "A real job like Aaron has, right Mother?" I asked, all faux innocence. "Tell us, Aaron, any marriage prospects on the horizon? We mustn't let the North line die with us, brother."

Mother's gaze snapped to me. "I'm not sure I like your tone, Asher."

She had no quibble with the pretentious, out-of-date words coming out of my mouth, just the tone in which I said them.

Aaron's body language expressed revenge at a later

date. Then he softened as he swiveled to address the lady of the manor—a title we'd never dare use to her face. "Actually, I have met someone. Her name is Beverly, and we met at work."

"Not one of your clients, I hope."

Because no one of good breeding would be in need of a lawyer according to mother.

"Not one of mine, no," Aaron hedged.

She took a dainty bite of risotto. "When can I meet her?"

Aaron shot a look my way. Not sure what he wanted me to do. Mother had her sights on him like a hawk with a field mouse.

Aaron reached up and ran a finger along his collar, pulling the material away from his throat. "We, uh, aren't at the meet-the-family stage of our relationship yet."

Mother frowned, the creases in her forehead deepening. "Meeting the parents is the first step. How else will you know if she's good enough for you? For this family?"

"As if anyone could be," I muttered.

"I know I taught you better than to mumble, Asher." Mother set her disapproving gaze on me. "If you have something to say, enunciate each word."

Aaron caught my eye. Shook his head. My peacekeeping brother didn't want a scene.

"Yes, ma'am." I shoveled in a spoonful of risotto, the food on my plate diminishing by half. *Fine dining* was just a synonym for teeny-tiny portions. One reason I'd stuffed myself on tacos before even driving over here.

"Bring her to dinner Friday at seven sharp." Mother placed her napkin beside her plate, signaling the meal was finished. "No excuses."

Aaron dipped his head, but not before I saw the tick in his jaw. Mother was formidable, but Aaron hadn't received his reputation in the courtroom by losing arguments. If he didn't want the two ladies to meet, he could spin the best excuse without Mother even realizing what he was doing. One of the reasons he remained her favorite. She couldn't see through him like she could me.

"Shall we retire to the verandah for a digestif?" Her heels clicked against the marble floor as she exited the dining hall and moved through the study. She didn't bother to look back to see if her sons followed. She'd raised us with a firm hand that expected obedience. Age didn't erase those expectations for Cynthia North.

While my brother continued in her wake toward the French doors leading to the balcony, I paused in the room where my father used to spend the majority of his time. Dark mahogany wood-paneled walls and deep, navy-blue wingback chairs sat over an antique Persian rug. The room still faintly smelled of his favorite pipe tobacco, floral and spicy.

I looked to the far wall. To a painting that had hung between two built-in bookcases for as long as I could remember. I'd asked my father once why he had the painting and he'd told me it was an investment. One day, that work of art would be worth a lot of money. Maybe my nine-year-old brain had been curious how some paint and brush strokes could equal wealth, but I'd found myself in this same spot often, staring at the framed artistry.

A portrait of Jesus and a small child. The way He looked at the child had captivated me. Maybe because neither of my own parents had ever looked at me with such a loving and open expression. It was why I was so drawn to the imagery of God as our Father, even now as an adult. Maybe that was why I could forge my own path, going against my parents' wishes and turning my back on a lifestyle that would garner their approval. Because I'd learned it didn't matter what they thought of me; I couldn't make decisions based on their opinions. There was Someone else whose approval mattered more. And even though I knew He loved me no matter what, there was no greater joy than the whisper I heard in my soul: *You are My son; I am well pleased with you.*

My fingers brushed the polished frame, then I walked out of the room. If I tarried any longer, Mother's lips would purse in disapproval again, and she already hated the life lines deepening there. She'd blame me if they grew even more pronounced.

I stepped out onto the balcony overlooking the Pacific Ocean. The coast curved in a crescent, jagged cliffs rising out of the sandy beach below. A million-dollar view, some would say, although my parents had paid much more than that for this manor on the hill. The smell of the ocean, briny and sharp, and the sound of the waves crashing, the tide's ebb and flow, spoke peace into my core.

Mother returned inside and came back a few minutes later with a glass tumbler an inch full of sherry in one hand and an identical glass of ice water in the other. She handed me the water. "If you could turn that into wine, then maybe you wouldn't need that real job after all."

She fixed her gaze out over the endless horizon. Aaron approached the railing on my other side, cradling a glass of amber liquid. Port, if I had to guess.

I took a sip of water, the cold liquid charting a path down my throat. I licked my lips. Standing in front of an audience in the thousands didn't make me nervous at all, but extending an invitation for one more to join that number made my knees clang together like tambourine zills. "I wanted to tell you...or ask you, rather. Umm...what I mean to say is..."

"What did I tell you earlier, Asher? Enunciate."

I exhaled. "My band is going on tour, and our last venue is here locally. I want to invite you to come and hear us play, Mother. Hear me, that is."

Her hand paused, her glass halfway to her lips. "You've never invited me to hear you play before."

"I didn't think you wanted to," I admitted in a whisper.

She considered. Behind her ice-blue eyes I could see her weighing the pros and cons of accepting. She'd soften and then instantly stiffen.

I held my breath, almost afraid to hope.

Her spine snapped rigid. I had my answer before she even opened her mouth.

"I'm sorry. I cannot condone your life choices, and my presence at one of your concerts" —she spat the word as a vulgarity—"would only send the message that I support the path you are traveling, and that is something I can never do."

I shot back the rest of the ice water in one cold swig. I wasn't sure which chilled me more—the burn of the liquid or the woman who was supposed to love me unconditionally turning her back on me yet again because I didn't meet her expectations.

No matter. I couldn't let my actions—my life—be determined and directed by pleasing others. I had to keep telling myself that. Even if the rejection of my family stabbed like a knife to the heart.

9

Betsy

"*H*ow much do you think it's killing Jocelyn that she can't design and make your dresses?" I asked, standing outside the bridal boutique's dressing rooms. "Or that she couldn't even be here to see you try the gowns on?"

A well-known fashion designer in New York had flown Jocelyn across the country after seeing some of her designs that Amanda had posted on the social media pages she'd created for Jocelyn's new business. Jocelyn had group texted us all the night before, her excitement pulsing in each letter and exclamation mark she'd used.

New York is amazing!!!!!!

I've never seen so much fabric, daring designs, and creativity in one place!!!!!

Will I wake up in the morning and realize it had all been a dream?!?!?

We'd assured her the dream was real and coming true. That the world had finally realized what we'd known all along—the brilliance of Jocelyn Dormus.

"She called me this morning and made me swear on the lives of the last remaining Javon rhinos that we'd send her pictures of every dress we try on." Nicole's muffled voice came from the other side of the white velvet curtain. She grumbled something under her breath.

"Need help in there?" Molly offered.

"This is dumb. I've already had a wedding once. If Drew weren't being so stubborn, we could be married already. A few hours' drive to Vegas and badda bing, badda boom, married."

"Since when do you channel the spirit of John Stamos as Uncle Jesse?" Amanda raised her voice so she could be heard from the adjoining changing room. "Drew's being stubborn for *you*, Nicole. You never had the wedding of your dreams because your mother guilted you into using the money to save the planet instead of letting you have one day when you could focus on yourself and not be some environmental hero. You've found the man of your dreams, and he wants you to have the wedding you deserve." She opened her curtain. "Now get out here so we can see you in that dress."

Molly covered her mouth with her hands, her eyes instantly misting as she stared at Amanda. *Athletic and willowy* the sales clerk had announced of Amanda's body type, then had helped them pick out a form-fitting number with a halter top and intricate beading down the bodice and hips.

"You look stunning," Molly finally managed to say.

Amanda looked down as she ran a hand over the corseted waist, a pinch forming between her brows. "You think so?"

The hooks holding the curtain to its rod rattled as Nicole pushed the white fabric to the side and stepped out. "I look like a poufy cloud. And not in a good way."

"Is there a good way to look like a cloud?" I drolled.

"You look…" Molly considered Nicole in the yards and yards of tulle falling around her. The shape of the dress did nothing to accentuate Nicole's figure. In fact, all the extra material did was hide the generous curves she possessed.

"Ethereal." Molly landed on a word to describe the dress and Nicole in it without hurting her feelings.

"You look like a cautionary tale."

Molly snapped her gaze at me, censure written in every frown line. Amanda appeared to be holding back a laugh.

"What? You're Mrs. Truth." I challenged Molly to argue with me. "Are you really going to say this is the dress Nicole should walk down the aisle in?"

"I wouldn't say that…" Molly hedged.

We all looked at her. Waited. Finally, she threw her hands up in the air. "Fine. I've been trying to work on tact because everyone keeps telling me I can be honest and not brutal about it, but you want the unedited truth? The sales woman is completely insane if she thinks that's the kind of silhouette that will flatter your figure. It looks like a white, gauzy potato sack, and I'm mad at her on your behalf." She crossed her arms and pouted. "Happy now?"

Amanda threw her arms around Molly and squeezed. "You don't have to edit yourself on our account. Be authentically you."

It hadn't been too long ago that Molly had lost her job because of her honesty policy. She'd had to take a nanny position to one of her former preschool students. It had been a hard time in her life, but everything had worked out. Especially considering she was now married to that student's father.

Nicole exhaled a deep breath. "I'm so relieved."

Molly tilted her head, confused.

"I'm not usually self-conscious about my shape or weight, but every woman has their moments of insecurity," Nicole confided. "If this dress was the best there was for me then—"

"Take it off," I interrupted. Whatever Nicole was going to say to finish that sentence didn't need to be voiced. I placed my hands on her shoulders and forcibly turned her to face the changing room, then shoved her inside.

I pivoted to Amanda. "You too. Take it off."

"But Molly said the dress is stunning," Amanda argued.

"*You* are stunning," I countered. "Do you really love this dress?" I waved my hand down the length of her. "Because you look uncomfortable to me. Your shoulders are hunched like Quasimodo, and your eyes are squinting like you're trying to hide pain."

She reached up and touched the knot of silky material at the base of her neck. "The halter is putting pressure on my spine and giving me a headache."

I pointed to the open dressing room. Nicole I could manhandle, no problem, but because of Amanda's chronic illness, I gave her a silent command and no-nonsense glower instead. I didn't want to unintentionally cause her pain.

She grinned, not the least bit intimidated by me, and retreated back to the changing room.

Sierra, Nicole's preteen daughter, sat in one of the plush chairs halfway between the dressing area and the half-circle of mirrors creating crescents around pedestals brides could step up on to inspect dresses from every angle. She had a pale rose-pink confection draped across her lap, the maid-of-honor dress she'd looked radiant in the moment the zipper had been fastened in the back. Nicole had tried to beg off any more shopping after mopping her face with a tissue at the sight of Sierra in that gown, claiming the day already a success, but I'd be hanged if either of my friends left this boutique without the gown of her dreams.

"Sierra." I tapped her on the shoulder. "Want to help pick out your mom's wedding dress?"

Her eyes lit. "Can I really?"

"Who knows her better than you? I bet you can pick out a gown that will make your mom cry."

Sierra's button nose scrunched. "We want her to cry?"

I steered her toward a wall of gowns whose hems almost grazed the ground. "We most certainly do. Molly." I looked over my shoulder.

Molly held up her cell phone. "Jocelyn and I are already on it." She pulled a lace-covered number off the rack and held the phone out. After a minute, she returned the dress.

Amanda was covered.

I went back to where Sierra stood struggling to separate the densely hung gowns so she could look at one.

"So," I said. "What kind of dress do you think your mom would like?"

She bit the corner of her bottom lip. "Well, I know a lot of people want to feel like a princess on their wedding day."

"Some do. Does your mom?"

Her shoulders lifted then fell. "I think she secretly wants to feel…" Her eyes darted around the room. She rose on her tiptoes and cupped a hand around her mouth as if she were sharing a secret. "Sexy," she whispered as her plump cheeks turned a deep scarlet.

I looked into Sierra's eyes and grinned. "I couldn't agree more."

We bypassed the ballgowns and headed to a section of dresses that would only be described as slinky. Form-fitting numbers that were more fit for a princess of the ocean than one living in a castle. I pushed all the gowns to one side, then slowly went through them one by one. I paused on a pearl-white gown with a feminine floral lace overlay, a key-hole back, and the illusion of a plunging neck line.

Sierra's breath caught, and I looked down at her. "This one?"

She nodded.

"I think so too."

Molly also had a dress draped over her arm as we approached the dressing room from opposite ends of the boutique.

"What did you find?" she asked.

The hem of the dress fell to the floor as I held up the top by the hanger. Molly's eyes widened.

"You?"

She lowered her arm, and the skirt of the dress cascaded to pool on the carpet. I reached out and fingered the material. Satin. Without a bead or flounce or applique in sight. The thing would probably feel like air on. Perfect for Amanda.

Molly and I grinned at each other.

"Are you guys done yet? It's getting cold standing here in my underwear," Amanda complained.

"Here you go." Molly thrust the dress past the curtain.

"I've got yours too, Nicole."

Nicole's hand shot out, and I put the gown in her open palm.

"I can't wear this!" she shrieked a moment later.

"Yes, you can. I'll help with the zipper."

"It's not the zipper I'm worried about!"

"Please, Mom," Sierra begged. "I picked it out for you."

Nicole sighed. "I'll try it on for you, but you might want to start looking for another dress. Maybe one a little, uh, bigger."

Sierra looked at me. I shook my head. There wouldn't be a need to find any more dresses for Nicole or Amanda to try on. Those two were perfect for them.

"How are you all doing?" The attendant supposed to be the expert floated over to us with a disingenuous customer service smile on her lips.

"We're fine, thank you." *No thanks to you.* I returned her false good humor by pushing the corners of my mouth up.

"Can I pick out any more gowns for you ladies?" She stopped between the two changing rooms.

The curtain to one, and then both, opened.

"Oh my. Those aren't the dresses we chose. Did I put y'all into the wrong rooms?" She looked as if she were trying to frown but physically couldn't. "I'm sorry for the mix up. I'll go grab the right gowns and get you two in them in a jiffy."

Yes. Go, I mentally commanded. *Get out of here.*

Amanda was blinking rapidly, her hand fanning her face while Nicole stood as if stunned, unable to speak.

"These are the ones." Molly spoke what I'd already known. "Let me take pictures for Jocelyn." She moved around the brides-to-be in a circle, snapping photos with her phone while dashing away tears with the back of her hand.

Nicole moved to the mirrors and pedestal first. Stepping up on the riser, she inspected herself in the reflection from all angles.

"Do you like it?" Sierra asked tentatively.

"I can't believe it's me," Nicole murmured.

The dress fit like it had been made for her; every line, every curve. The dress was bold and unapologetic. Everything Nicole embodied. Instead of trying to quiet or hide her like the first dress had, this one gave Nicole an air of power and self-confidence that did indeed make her look sexy as anything.

A sob shook Nicole's shoulders.

Sierra's gaze shot to mine. "We made her cry!" she shouted in triumph.

Nicole's sniffle turned to a snicker. She pulled her daughter into her arms for a big hug.

"No more giving Drew grief about having a real wedding," I mock-lectured. "You wear that gown and you make him eat his heart out."

Amanda mounted the platform next to Nicole's. She looked classy and elegant. Timeless.

"This is the softest thing I have ever had on my skin," she said in awe.

"Just wait until the wedding night. Peter won't be able to keep his hands off you." Molly winked.

"Can we please remember the young ears in our midst?" Nicole scowled.

Sierra giggled.

The bell over the entrance clanged, signaling a new customer.

Good. Maybe the sales clerk with no taste would remain occupied.

Amanda splayed her hands over her thighs. She met my eyes through the mirror. Her chest rose and fell beneath the sweetheart neckline. "I want to ask you something, Betsy, and I really want you to say yes."

Unease wound its way between my ribs. Amanda's nervousness made my finger twitch.

Ridiculous. She was one of my best friends. Of course I'd say yes to anything she asked if it was in my power to grant her request. I'd do anything for my friends.

"I…" She licked her lips. "I want you to sing at my wedding."

A high-pitched ringing filled my ears.

"You have such a gorgeous voice," she rushed on. "I don't know why you don't let other people hear you sing. Is it stage fright? I don't want to make you do something if you really don't want to, but it would mean so, so much to me if you could sing 'Bless the Broken Road' when Peter and I have our first dance as husband and wife. Please?"

Blood rushed through my limbs, leaving me tingly and off-center. "I…"

I didn't know what to say.

Where was a snarky quip when I needed one most?

10

Asher

I wasn't sure what had possessed me to walk into that bridal boutique. I'd seen Betsy through the glass window as I was walking down the sidewalk, and next thing I knew, the little bell above the door rang a greeting as the scent of some sort of fragrant flower wafted over me.

I couldn't explain it. I wasn't the kind of person who ducked his head when they saw someone they knew in public, pretending to have not noticed them to avoid small talk, but I also didn't go out of my way to intercept the person either. Especially not by walking into a store catering exclusively to the opposite gender. I was about as out of place among all the white fluffy material and bridal mannequins as a tuba in a string quartet.

But I hadn't been able to help myself. I'd seen her,

laughing with some other women, the serious expression usually forced into place on her face erased. I'd wondered what Betsy would look like if she lost some of her rigidity and smiled. Not her cynical curve of the lips. Not even that satisfied professional smile that had taken me off guard during our first rehearsal with her, but a real, honest-to-goodness, Betsy-with-her-guard-down smile.

I hadn't been prepared for its force. Seeing Betsy smile had the same effect as a meteor crashing into me, knocking me off course, sucking me into her gravitational pull, and locking me into her orbit. My feet had grown a will of their own and propelled me toward the wedding dress shop door.

"Can I help you with something, sir?" A young woman in a pantsuit approached, a polite expression on her face.

"No, thank you. I just—" Just what? Suddenly became a stalker in the last fifteen seconds? Had an aneurysm that cut off communication between my brain and lower limbs? Lost my grip on all common sense?

I had no way to explain my presence in this shop. Not to this employee and certainly not to Betsy if she turned around for whatever reason and spotted me here. The best plan would be to hightail it out of there before Betsy was any the wiser. I could pretend the whole thing never happened. I'd deal with whatever revelation I seemed to have had on the sidewalk later, in private. Although, I wasn't sure what I could do about that either.

"You have such a gorgeous voice," one of the women with Betsy was saying. She leaned forward in a dress of classic simplicity and elegance, her eyes searching while her tone pleaded. "I don't know why you don't let other people hear you sing. Is it stage fright?"

Stage fright. Why hadn't I thought of that? If a fear of singing for an audience held Betsy back, maybe I could help her overcome her anxiety.

"I don't want to make you do something if you really don't want to, but it would mean so, so much to me if you could sing 'Bless the Broken Road' when Peter and I have our first dance as husband and wife. Please?"

I held my breath. I should go. So I wouldn't be spotted, yes, but also because now I'd stepped my oversized feet across the line into eavesdropping territory. But my brain-limb connection hadn't been repaired, and my feet refused to obey what common sense I had left. If anything, I strained forward, trying to hear Betsy's response with about as much anticipation as a rockhead at his first Rolling Stones concert.

"I…" Betsy started and then stopped.

You what?! I wanted to scream. I took a step forward. My shoulder bumped something hard. Out of the corner of my eye, I registered a mannequin in a ball gown teetering and shot my hand out to steady her. She landed in my arms like a swooning miss out of an Austen novel.

Of course, all the racket may as well have been a spotlight directed straight at me.

"Asher?" Betsy said my name with incredulity.

I brought the plastic woman in my arms out of a dip fit for a ballroom and set her on her feet, awkwardly patting her shoulder. Why? Couldn't say. Apparently today was filled with things that I did without any rhyme or reason.

"What are you doing here?" Incredulity gave way to suspicion.

Still hadn't come up with a good answer for that question.

"Do you know him?" The same bride who'd asked Betsy to sing at her wedding posed this question as well.

"He's the lead singer of the band I'm working with."

I stepped forward confidently, not at all like I'd just been caught essentially spying on an employee. "Asher North. Nice to meet you all." I held the gaze of each of Betsy's friends. They responded with varying degrees of interest and caution.

Betsy cocked a hip. "In the market for a wedding dress? Or always a bridesmaid and never a bride, Asher? Hmm?" She quirked a saucy brow.

I grinned sheepishly and ran a hand along the back

of my neck. "I, uh, saw you through the window and thought I'd say hi."

She absorbed that but didn't appear pleased. "Why?"

Another fantastic question. "Because that's what friendly people do when they see someone they know."

She blew out a breath. "Fine. Hi." She waved one hand and then immediately waved the other. "Bye."

"Betsy!" a small blonde, the only other woman not in a wedding dress, exclaimed.

"What?"

"You're being rude," she said out of the side of her mouth while maintaining her pleasant expression and soft smile.

"So?" Betsy responded to her friend but hadn't taken her eyes off me, the same challenge she always directed my way deep within her caramel-colored irises.

I broke eye contact and turned my focus to the trio of friends and the preteen girl. "I'm sorry if I intruded on your special day. May I say, though, that you ladies look ravishing in those gowns. Be careful. Walking down the aisle looking as breathtaking as you two do may be liable to make the grooms so tongue-tied that they forget how to even say I do."

The young girl giggled. "We have to be careful with him, right, Mom? That's what you said about sweet talkers."

The first bride's grin grew like a crescendo. "And look at her now, marrying her very own." She stepped off the platform she'd been on and offered me her hand to shake. "I'm Amanda, by the way. This is Molly." She pointed to the blonde. "Sierra." The girl waved shyly. "And Nicole." The second woman in a wedding dress acknowledged me with a head tilt.

"Betsy may not be showing it, but she's relieved you're here." Amanda had mischief written all over her face.

I whipped my gaze back to Betsy. She'd adopted a bored expression. If she was feeling anything, relief or otherwise, she hid it well.

"See, she thinks she's gotten out of answering my question. Thinks I've forgotten about it entirely, but I haven't. Not the question nor the intervention she participated in on my behalf not that long ago."

Betsy pressed her lips together. "You were hiding something, and it was for your own good. Because we care about you."

Amanda didn't back down. "So are you and so is this. We love you, Bets. Tell us why you won't sing when your voice is better than most of the people we hear on the radio."

"It really is," Molly whispered her agreement.

I nodded my head, almost afraid to remind them I was there. The same question I'd asked myself since the moment I'd heard her unique, soulful voice released into the atmosphere. I held my breath, almost as if the answer meant something to me personally—more than what her singing could bring to the band. I couldn't explain it. Why whatever would come out of her mouth next meant so much. But I felt as if I stood on a precipice and my fate rested on what Betsy would say.

Silly. Emotional. Overreactive. All things artistic types were accused of being. But I couldn't help it. How did one make themselves feel things less? And did I really want to?

Betsy swung her gaze to me, an internal argument warring behind her eyes.

If I weren't here, would she open up to her friends? Obviously, whatever her reasoning for keeping her gift to herself, it was something difficult for her to talk about. Why else would these ladies who clearly knew and loved her so well not be privy to the root of her logic?

No matter how curious I was…

No, that wasn't right. It was more than curiosity. A need, really. But how could that be?

Even so, no matter how much I thought I needed to know, I'd step aside if it meant Betsy would share her heart or fear or whatever it was with someone. Especially people who were safe and cared for her.

"I've clearly intruded," I said, taking a backward step. "It was nice to meet you all. I hope to see you again sometime."

Betsy rolled her eyes and sighed. "Stop acting like I'm the Grinch and just stole all your Christmas presents, Cindy Lou Who." She lowered her voice and muttered. "Maybe if you learn the truth, you'll finally stop pestering me and leave me alone."

"What truth, Bets?" Nicole asked.

"It's no big deal, really." Betsy shifted her weight over her feet and gave a small laugh meant to dispel the seriousness that had begun to collect on the air like morning dew on a pre-dawn lawn.

Her efforts were in vain. If anything, her friends' focus zeroed in on her even further, her humorless chuckle more a flag saying to dig deeper than a red herring likely to get them off the scent.

"If it's no big deal, then why haven't you ever told us before? Is it why you have that silly rule against dating musicians?" Molly asked.

"It's not a silly rule." Betsy sniffed. "But yes, if you must know."

"How's everything going over here?" The sales clerk chose that moment to make an appearance. "Can I help you out of those dresses or make another gown selection for you?"

"No!"

"We're fine!"

"Go away!"

I wasn't sure who'd said what, but the outbursts like foghorns in the night made the attendant scamper to the back of the store faster than a runaway bride with a new pair of Nikes.

"You were saying?" Molly demurred as if nothing had happened.

Betsy shrugged again like her revelation wouldn't be a big deal. "Musicians are selfish, egotistical people only out for themselves and their dreams without a thought or care for anyone they may step on or hurt along their way to the top."

I waited for her to look at me and at least tack on a *no offense* or *present company excluded* or *something*— anything, really, that would exempt me from the same box that she heaped everyone else with any musical aspirations into, the lid hammered closed with nails of her judgement.

The look never came. Nor any kind of space I could mentally manipulate to maneuver myself into a more feasible light in her eyes. No, to her I was one of *them*. Said with a sneer, derision, and heaping amounts of condescension.

She looked down at her nails, but she couldn't keep up the act of nonchalance for long. She curled her fingers into fists. "I don't want to be with someone like that, and I definitely don't want to become that type of person." She tried to brush her shoulders in a *c'est la vie* attitude, but no one standing in that shop believed it wasn't a big deal to Betsy.

"Why do you think—" My voice croaked, clogged with so many emotions. I couldn't say I wasn't hurt, because I was. But upon closer inspection, the ache spreading across my chest was more for her than the barbed accusations she'd tossed my way.

Betsy hadn't struck me as a particularly prejudiced

person. Snarky, sure, but that had more to do with her hilarious dry sense of humor than any real ill will toward people. Which meant, if she truly felt this way about people in the music industry, she had to have a reason. And the only reasons I could think of were rooted in personal pain.

She pushed her curly mass of hair away from her face. "I didn't always. But I've learned from my mistake. The consequences—" She squeezed her eyes shut. When she opened them, the wall of indifference had been erected once more.

She pivoted to face Amanda. "You asked if I'd sing at your wedding, and I'm honored by the request." She swallowed hard, every word costing her. "Even though I've made a personal vow not to sing in public, for you" —she looked around at her friends—"for all of you, I'd do anything. So, if you want me to sing, then I will sing."

Amanda squealed and threw herself into Betsy's arms. Molly, Nicole, and Sierra joined them in a group hug. I almost blurted out how the song was beautiful as a duet but managed to bite my tongue just in time.

There was more to the story than Betsy had been willing to tell. She'd cut herself off from saying the rest, and I couldn't help but wonder, what else had happened?

Either way, I knew what I was going to do. Betsy had been silently challenging me from the very first moment we'd met—a test I had no intention of failing.

I'd prove to Betsy that all of her assumptions about musicians in general and me in particular needed to be rewritten. We didn't all fit into the outline she'd given us.

I'm going to change your mind, Betsy Vargas. Just see if I don't.

Betsy

I stared down at my bed, clothes in neat piles across the striped bedspread, an outfit for each day of the week. Hopefully someone in Asher's band had thought about the need for a laundromat every once in a while, because I didn't own enough clothes to last the whole tour without doing laundry. Hotels usually had facilities, but Asher had informed me that he'd rented a bus for both transportation and lodging purposes.

For the band's own safety, no one had better snore. After hours of being kept awake by obnoxious breathing noises, I wouldn't put it past myself to consider a pillow a weapon. Just a little suffocation until rendered unconscious. That wouldn't be going too far, would it?

A light tapping sounded on my door.

"Come in."

Bella paused at the threshold, Charlotte on her hip. My niece had her fist in her mouth, baby drool hanging in long strands off her lips, her tiny fingers wet and shiny. Bella came in and sat on the edge of the mattress, transferring Charlotte to her lap. Charlotte lunged for the buffalo plaid flannel folded on top of the closest stack. Bella caught her but not before the infant fisted the flannel and brought a sleeve to her mouth.

Essence of baby. The perfect man repellant. Maybe I should've gotten Charlotte to gum all of my shirts for extra protection. I trusted myself, but…

Yeah, it was that *but* that I was worried about. I'd told Asher what I thought of musicians. He hadn't protested. Hadn't gotten defensive or tried to argue with my assessment. But he also hadn't backed away. If anything, he seemed to have stepped up. To the line or the gauntlet or whatever it was he thought I'd thrown down.

I wasn't scared.

Cautious wasn't scared. It was being smart.

"Are you excited?" Bella asked.

I gave her my patented *girl, please* look.

She laughed as I'd intended.

"Silly me. I forgot you don't get excited about anything."

I hiked a shoulder to my ear. I had the ability to feel excitement, I just didn't get effusive over every little thing like some people.

Bella hid a yawn behind the back of her hand.

"Charlotte still have her nights and days mixed up?" I ran a finger over the baby's knuckles.

"I think she's teething. I went to the store today and picked up a teething ring, some Tylenol, and gel to put on her gums. Hopefully those things will help."

"Want me to take her so you can go get a nap?"

Bella rested her chin on Charlotte's fine brown fuzz of hair and grinned up at me. "I want you to tell me all the fun things you're about to do so I can live vicariously through you."

"I'll be working, Bell, not going on some grand adventure."

She pushed out her bottom lip. "Spoil sport."

I folded a pair of jeans and laid them beside the cotton cactus-print bottoms and vintage tee I'd gotten at Borrego Springs years ago that I planned to wear for pajamas.

Bella tilted her chin toward me. "Are you afraid…" She paused, tripping over her words. "Are you afraid that you'll end up like me?"

My hands stilled, denim tangled in my fingers.

My sister pulled her daughter closer. Bent her head and snuggled her cheek next to Charlotte's. "If I could go back in time," she said softly as she looked up and caught my eyes with her own, "I wouldn't change a thing."

Pregnant at sixteen. A single mother. Abandoned by the guy who'd said all kinds of sweet words to convince her he loved her, that they'd be together forever.

That had lasted about as long as it had taken for the second line to appear on the pee-on-a-stick drugstore test.

I'd witnessed her tender heart shatter. The wails of her wondering what she'd done wrong for Wyatt to leave. What made her unlovable? Her midnight worries of a child having a child. How would she finish high school? Should she keep her baby or consider giving her up for adoption? What would their parents think?

My baby sister's heart had lain in a million pieces, and it had all been my fault. Wyatt had come into my studio to record a demo. He'd had a quick wit and seemed more down to earth and mature than other guys his age. He'd had a plan outside of music. College with a degree that would provide him with a steady job, because he knew there were people more talented than he trying to break into the industry, so the statistics were against him.

It had been love at first sight for Bella, and I'd thought the feelings were mutual. The way Wyatt had looked at my sister was the stuff of romance novels. But in the end, he'd shown his true colors. He was like every other guy with dreams of grandeur that outshone anything else in their lives. When it came down to the bottom line, he'd only looked out for number one, and that hadn't been Bell or their unborn child.

"I'm serious, Bets." Bella sounded earnest.

I set down the pair of socks I'd been folding to give her my full attention. Why did she want to talk about this now? She couldn't go back and change things, even if she wouldn't. Although, I would in a heartbeat. I'd tell that charming *idioto* to get lost and never come back. Make sure he and my sister never set eyes on one another.

"If things had been different, then I wouldn't have Charlotte." Bella kissed the crown of her daughter's head. "And I can't imagine my life without her now."

I sighed and sat beside them, the mattress compressing under my weight and making her lean toward me. I wrapped my arms around them. "I love you both, *hermana.*"

She rested the back of her head on my shoulder. "What I'm trying to say is, don't be scared to live your life. You aren't going to make the same mistakes I did." She sat up and twisted to face me, a mischievous gleam in her eye. "You can have fun making your own."

I frowned at her, even though my lips twitched to smile. "I'm never scared." I stood and retrieved two more socks, folding them together. "And I don't plan on making any mistakes, thank you very much."

"I forget that you're perfect." She smirked as she plucked the socks out of my hands and tossed them at my face. "Let's see how well that works out for you."

Charlotte started to fuss, so Bella left to try and get her down for a nap. I hauled my suitcase from the closet and transferred my neat stacks into the luggage, sitting on the top to get the zipper all the way around.

Papi popped his head through the doorway. "All set?"

I looked around my room in search of anything I may have forgotten. "I think so."

He came in and collected my suitcase, carrying it down the stairs for me and setting it by the front door.

"We're so proud of you, mija," he said as he pulled me into a side hug and pressed a kiss to my temple. "And I want you to know, I contacted a lawyer. The paperwork to reunite your cousin Camilla with the family has been filed." His eyes glistened with emotion. "It is a good thing, what you have done for your family."

I took a mental snapshot. When I was on the road somewhere, maybe in a dive in the middle of nowhere on the way to Vegas or dealing with some crisis or another to get the show going—because these things were more a question of *when* than *if*—I'd pull out this picture and remind myself of the reason I was doing this in the first place.

More hugs were given and received, then I was sent off with a plastic container filled with fresh, home-made empanadas filled with ground beef, spices, fresh herbs, green olives, and boiled eggs. Mami probably expected me to share since she'd packed so many. I'd have to give that some careful consideration, since her empanadas were the best thing anyone could ever put in their mouth. It would be a truly selfless act to share.

The smell seeping past the lid tempted me as I drove the fifteen miles to the church. We were all supposed to meet there, load the equipment and instruments onto the rented bus, then head out. The itinerary placed us at the farthest away venue first, then slowly making our way back with each performance.

As I neared the church, the sun reflected off a shiny silver monstrosity. Actually, I take it back. Shiny didn't even begin to describe this behemoth on wheels. It was blinding, both literally and metaphorically. I shielded my eyes as I turned into the parking lot, afraid the brightness would cause me to lose my vision and crash into the flowering tree planted near the curb. The thing looked like Dr. Frankenstein had turned in his lab coat for mechanic coveralls. Part lunar vehicle, part post-apocalypse getaway ride.

I pulled into a parking space and killed the engine. I had no reason to linger in my car. Unfortunately. I took one more whiff of Mami's empanadas before I forced myself to open the car door and face my fate for the next few weeks. What did sixty years of people in a tin can smell like? I had a feeling I was about to find out.

Dave came out of the church carrying a snare drum, Marcus right behind him with a cymbal stand in each hand. They disappeared around the other side of the bus.

I popped the trunk and retrieved my suitcase, next going around to the passenger side to get the food Mami had shoved in my hands. Tricia saw me and waved me over. She stood off to the side of the bus, away from the guys moving Dave's drum set piece by piece.

She touched her wrist to her forehead. "Can you believe how warm it is today? I know I should be used to the weather by now, but eighty degrees in February always surprises me."

A bee buzzed by and landed on a camellia blooming in the landscaping along the church's exterior. The trailing nasturtiums and poppies that flowered by the highways as well as the few planted pear trees in the neighborhoods tricked people of Southern California into thinking it was spring when other parts of the country were still experiencing snow storms and below-freezing temperatures.

"The Santa Ana winds up from the desert do tend to bring these higher temperatures, but the forecast says it's supposed to cool back down to the low seventies and even high sixties again in a few days."

She stretched her back, eyeing the bus with wariness. "What are the chances, do you think, that thing has air conditioning?"

Probably not as good as us getting tetanus if we scratched ourselves on any of its surfaces. Instead of answering, I opened the lid of the Tupperware and held the container in front of Tricia. "Empanada?"

"Oh." She seemed surprised but lifted a meat-filled pastry from where it nestled among the others and took a bite. A moan emanated from behind her closed lips. "This is so good." Her eyes went wide when she opened them. "Did you make these?"

I shook my head. "My mom."

She shoved the rest in her mouth and thumbed the corner of her lips, chewing and nodding her head. She'd closed her eyes again. Mami would love her and how she made food a full body experience.

I placed the container in her hands. "Have as many as you want. I'm going to help with the loading." I didn't want the mixing board to just be thrown in without any care. Those things could be fragile. We also didn't want to get to another city and discover that the in-ear monitors had been left behind. Then there were the cables. I definitely didn't want them all to get mixed up or knotted together. I had Velcro tapes to keep the TRS, TS, RCA, and all the cable connectors organized.

As I stepped into the sanctuary, Asher was bent over an amplifier. He stood, lifting the black box, his muscles cording under the tight hem of his T-shirt.

Caray. My breath hitched. *Look away, Betsy*, I told myself.

Why? You can't unsee his sculpted physique. Amanda's voice in my head this time, the shameless flirt.

Ah! I pulled my gaze away, but Amanda in my head was right. Even when I blinked, Asher's form highlighted behind my eyelids. I groaned. I did *not* need this. I needed the opposite of this. To stop noticing things about Asher. His long, tapered fingers and competent hands. His deep, penetrating gaze that seemed to strip away the layers and leave me feeling exposed. His easy smile that tried to convince me to relax despite my misgivings. And now, a peek at physical strength—long, sinewy muscles that spoke of dedication and self-discipline. Which, because I wasn't a coward I'd be honest and admit, made my blood pool in a delicious heat in my belly.

I squared my shoulders and set my jaw. Traitorous body. Unlawful anatomy. Didn't it remember my number one rule? No. Falling. For. Musicians. Physical attraction was a stumbling block, but I would not be taken down that easily.

Asher set the amplifier down beside the others. He straightened, and our gazes locked across the room. His crooked smile lifted on one side of his face.

"Betsy, you're just the woman I've been waiting for."

12

Asher

*B*etsy's toe caught on the commercial-grade carpeting running under the many rows of chairs set up in the church's sanctuary instead of traditional pews. She managed to catch herself without falling, but the color traveling up her neck to her cheeks belied the unaffected expression she kept on her face out of what was probably sheer willpower.

It hadn't been the carpet that had tripped her up. It had been what I'd said. That she was the woman I'd been waiting for. If not for her physical stumble, I wouldn't have even heard what could've been considered a double entendre or second layer to what had come out of my mouth. Had I even meant it that way, on some subconscious level?

Betsy intrigued me, I'd admit. The more I got to know her, the more I wanted to know. She wasn't easy, but then, hard things had always drawn my interest.

Mostly because I'd always found they were more than worth the effort. A sweet reward not given to just anyone.

Not that I considered Betsy a reward. Heaven help me, if she even caught wind that her name and the equivalent of a trophy were tied together in a thought, she'd probably have my hide one way or another.

I grinned. The firecracker.

But I had to be careful. Not so much for my sake but for hers. She didn't trust. Me. Those in the music industry. People in general, probably. And that was something I'd have to earn. Prove to her that not everyone was like the person who had caused her so much pain in the past. That I wasn't like that. I could be patient when I needed to be.

I smiled again but turned my head and hid my grin in the crook of my shoulder lest Betsy see and get suspicious.

She'd find out just how persistently patient I could be.

I bent and picked up one of the amplifiers. They'd go in the back storage compartment under the bus in a neat row, bungie corded if necessary so they wouldn't shift too much on the road and get damaged. They weren't exactly light, but propelling my body up the faces of vertical cliffs had honed my muscles, so hefting these around wasn't too much of a workout.

An unintelligible sound emitted from Betsy's vicinity. Was that a squeak or a huff or a snort? None of those really described the surprising sound. I looked over my shoulder at her in time to catch the wave of her hair. As if she'd quickly whipped her head around in order to not be caught staring at me.

A satisfying warmth spread out from behind my breastbone almost to the point that I couldn't even feel the weight in my arms any longer. Was Betsy... attracted to me? Even if it was against her will?

I wanted to laugh but instead bit down on my tongue to keep myself in check. A chuckle then, at that precise moment, would do nothing to coax Betsy to my side. More like give her one more justification to not like "guys like me," as she put it. Because she'd know she'd been caught checking me out and think I was over here preening my ego. (Okay, maybe I was a little. But a beautiful woman who I found myself more attracted to every day was actually showing an ounce of interest. I don't think anyone could blame me for a teeny tiny mental fist-bump.)

She busied herself with coiling cords, and I passed by without a word. Dave was hunched inside the middle storage compartment of the bus, his arm popping out to take hold of a tom drum from Jimmy, when I made it to the parking lot. A few hours later, with everything packed and loaded and a sheen of sweat coating most of our brows, we were ready to go.

"Let's have a word of prayer before we head out." I extended my hands away from my sides, and the rest of the band shuffled forward to form a circle. Everyone except Betsy, who eyed us with as much skepticism as if I'd said let's form a circle and have a séance.

I let go of Marcus's hand and extended my fingers to Betsy. "I promise we won't sing 'Kumbaya.' I know how much you love that song."

She huffed but stepped forward. She eyed my inviting palm with wariness but then squared her shoulders and marched to my side, gripping my hand with the force of a businesswoman wanting to intimidate her competition in the boardroom.

I swallowed back my chuckle, then ever so lightly ran my thumb across the ridges of her knuckles. She sucked in a breath, and her fingers loosened like someone letting air out of a bicycle tire. I readjusted our hands to fit comfortably together. Snuggly.

When I looked up, she scowled at me. I smiled innocently in return, then closed my eyes.

"Father God, we thank You for this opportunity to use our voices and instruments to exalt Your name, and we pray that our efforts on this journey will bring glory to the kingdom and not to this world. Keep us safe on the roads, and go before us so the greatest good can be accomplished. Amen."

Hushed amens echoed mine. Betsy stared at me with her brow furrowed. She blinked, cleared her expression, then stormed past me.

My lips tipped in her wake.

Dave climbed into the driver's seat while Jimmy took shotgun. I waited for the other three to climb the stairs into the main body of the bus, then followed behind them. She wasn't the sleekest or most classy wheels on the road, but I'd gotten a good deal on the rental, and the owner assured me she was reliable. While the outside looked like something you'd see in a Dystopian blockbuster, the inside had been renovated in the last decade. Most importantly, it had six beds.

"This is not as awful as I'd imagined." Tricia's gaze swung around the space. She ran a hand along the tiny kitchen—mostly a miniature square sink, dollhouse-sized refrigerator, and a one-foot-by-one-foot block of counter space—before lowering herself onto the cushion of the banquette.

"Can I claim any of these beds?" Marcus called from farther back in the bus. There were three bunk beds two high—one on one side and two on the other.

"Leave one of the bottom bunks for me, please. That way I can just literally roll myself out of bed in the morning." Tricia grimaced from where she sat. "That might be the only way I'll heft my body out of there and not imitate a pathetic turtle that's flipped upside down on its shell and can't get itself up and walking again."

"Trish, if you—"

She held up a hand to stop me.

I sighed. "Okay, but please let me know if you change your mind. At any time. You know I'll buy you a plane ticket home. Just say the word."

Dave turned the key in the ignition, and the floor

started vibrating beneath our feet. "Let's get this show on the road." He pulled out of the church's parking lot and turned onto the street.

Betsy swayed with the motion, and I almost reached out to steady her in case she lost her balance and stumbled to the side, but then thought better of it. Maybe because I recognized the flimsy excuse for what it was: a thin justification to be close to her. To touch her. But if I jumped the gun and didn't bide my time to prove all the things I wanted to prove, then I'd never be able to be close or touch her on a deeper level. And although my body lit up with the idea of a physical connection—two live wires sparking on contact—my soul recognized and craved the rarity of a possibility of the greatest gift of a lifetime.

I just had to get her to trust me.

I slid into the banquette beside Trish. "How about a road trip game?"

"What are you thinking?" Jimmy turned in his seat to look back at us.

"How about Would You Rather?" I peeked over at Betsy out of the corner of my eye. She didn't really seem like a gaming type of person, but I hoped she'd play along. We had a long drive ahead of us.

Tricia pulled out the elastic band holding her hair back, then scratched her head in the spot her ponytail had been. "I'm in."

"Sounds fun." Jimmy grinned. "Marcus will play too."

"Do I have a choice?" Marcus's voice was muffled from the back of the bus.

"No," Jimmy answered.

We all looked to Betsy to see if she'd join our fun. Her dad wasn't here to make her, like Marcus's. She rolled her eyes and plopped onto the bench seat on the other side of Tricia.

"Who's going first?" Tricia asked.

"I have one for Marcus." Jimmy gripped the side of the captain chair he twisted in to be in on the game. "Would you rather only be able to respond in emojis or never be able to text again?"

Marcus looked up from his phone, where he'd clearly been in the middle of typing out a text. "Easy. Emojis."

Jimmy shook his head. "I don't even get what half those emojis mean." He'd lowered his voice to only project to the middle of the bus instead of all the way back to the sleeping area. "Or the way the kids use them. For instance, what does the guy in the suit levitating even mean? Or the octopus? Why does Marcus's girlfriend text him octopuses all the time? I don't get it."

"The octopus emoji means cuddles or a virtual hug," Betsy explained. "You don't have to worry until they start sending each other eggplant or peach emojis."

Jimmy's forehead folded into four horizontal lines. "Fruit and veggie emojis are bad? Why?"

Tricia cleared her throat. "I'll go next." Her upper

body squared toward me as she twisted at the waist. "Would you rather have seven fingers on each hand or seven toes on each foot?"

"Fingers," came my automatic reply.

Her brows rose. "Really? But you can hide extra toes in shoes."

"Yes, but can you imagine the songs I could make my guitar sing with seven fingers? It would be epic."

She snorted as she looked at me with the indulgence of an older sister. "Only you'd think about how having more fingers would improve your music."

I laughed. "Guilty." I rubbed my palms together. "Okay, my turn. Who should I ask? Hmm." My gaze rested on each person in turn. Jimmy—duck. Tricia—duck. Marcus—duck. Betsy. I grinned. Goose.

"Betsy, would you rather be able to travel back in time or be like Marty McFly and visit the future?"

Her body instantly stilled and her eyes rounded as if she'd been caught with her hand in the cookie jar. I'd hit a nerve with that question.

She swallowed. "I'll take a trip to the past for a thousand, Alex."

"How come?" I pressed. There was more to her answer than she let on.

She tsked. "Explaining one's answers isn't part of the game. I believe it's my turn now." She didn't miss a beat. "Jimmy, would you rather always get green lights at traffic stops but never find a parking spot or always get the best parking spot and hit every red light?"

Jimmy groaned. "That's a hard one."

We played a few more rounds before Jimmy complained about his back hurting from the odd angle he had to hold himself in to face us and switched positions in his seat to look out the windshield. Tricia pulled out her phone to text her husband. Apparently, he was just waking up wherever he was in the world, and she always liked to tell him good morning and that she loved him at the start of his day.

Betsy stood and shuffled toward the back of the bus. I should probably have gotten my notebook and pen from the messenger bag I'd set on one of the beds earlier. I still had a couple of songs I wanted to work on.

The bus swayed as I stood, and I reached out and pressed a palm to the cool window to balance myself. Once settled, I let go and strode down the narrow walkway in the center.

Betsy straightened, a book held to her chest. It was like being on an airplane and meeting another passenger going the opposite direction. There was no way we'd be able to cross paths without our bodies being pressed closer together than a peanut butter and jelly sandwich.

For the second time in less than an hour, I struggled with a part of myself that wanted to do something other than what I knew to be the smart and right thing. The part of me that wanted instant gratification urged me to stand my ground. Turn sideways so she could slip by, but use the proximity to my advantage. Maybe I could overwhelm her senses like she overwhelmed mine.

I shook my head. That was short-sighted, and I'd already committed to the long game. Besides, taking advantage of the situation and the tight space and pressing myself unwantedly upon her person—wasn't that what she expected "someone like me" to do? I couldn't prove anything with those actions.

Denying my desire to be close enough to breathe her in, for her to have no choice but to see me for who I was and not through the tainted filter in which she viewed me, I took a step back. I'd retreat until the space widened and she could walk past without even the hint of a graze between our bodies. My heat would not jump out to warm any part of her.

The bus lurched as if Dave had slammed on the brakes. Betsy's caramel eyes widened, and she pitched forward. I caught her, my arm coming around her waist and the palm of my hand pressing into the small of her back to offer support. The moment caused me to stumble, but I planted the ball of my foot into the floor and countered our balance while reaching one hand up to grip the rail a curtain was hung from to give the bunks privacy and block the light.

"Sorry about that." Dave called back. "Someone cut me off."

Betsy's hands were pinned between our chests, her brow level with my lips. If I moved my head at all, I'd be kissing her forehead. She looked up as if reading my thoughts, a frown on her face. I lowered my chin but miscalculated the distance between us. Our noses nuzzled together like Lady and the Tramp. My arms constricted. Time stood still.

Her palms pushed against my chest. Could she feel my heart knocking against my ribs?

"I know you liked the idea of seven fingers, but I'd be worried about the five you have if you don't let me go right this second."

My hands dropped to my side, and my cheek twitched as I held back a smile. Betsy may think her barbs had the potential to hurt me, but she was like a prickly pear cactus: a bit thorny on the outside but soft and sweet on the inside. And wouldn't you know, nopales tasted delicious on the tongue.

"Betsy." She'd only gone two steps when I softly said her name.

She turned—reluctantly, if the stiff set of her shoulders said anything.

"Another man would probably tease you about how you said you didn't fall for musicians, and yet you literally just did. But I'm not like other men, so instead, I'll say that no matter how many times you fall, I'll always be willing to catch you."

13

Betsy

*T*wo…three…four…

A choking sound interrupted my counting, followed by a deep exhalation. I rolled over onto my back and stared up at the ceiling less than two feet above my head. So far, the longest Tricia had gone without breathing was five seconds. I'd bolted up so fast thinking something was seriously wrong that I'd slammed my head into the overhead compartment. I'd be lucky if I didn't have a bruise the size of Texas along my hairline when I looked in the mirror in the morning. Sideswept bangs weren't the best look on me.

Tricia took another deep, rattling breath in, making as much noise as a lumberjack with his favorite chainsaw. Who knew if a tree falling in a forest made a sound? But a pregnant woman in a tour bus sure as anything did. If the racket were coming from one of the guys, the outcome of the night would have a

different ending, but, come to find out, I had boundaries, and contemplating homicide on a sweet pregnant
lady crossed those.

Tricia snorted, smacked her lips, then exhaled
loudly.

*That's it. I can't listen to this a second longer or I'll go
insane.* I grabbed my hoodie and pushed my feet into a
pair of slip-on canvas shoes. Tiptoeing a few steps
before asking myself what I was doing—Tricia made
enough noise to wake someone from a coma—I walked
the rest of the way to the door, then stepped out into
the cold night air. The temperature had to have
dropped at least twenty degrees since the sun went
down. Desert living for you.

I pulled the hoodie on over my head and yanked the
hem down, shoving my hands into the kangaroo pouch
in front. I should have thought to bring a heavier
jacket. Then again, I hadn't expected midnight strolls
just north of the Mojave Desert.

Not sure what I'd expected, really. While I'd been
hired to do live performances before, I'd never toured
with a band. Even then, I imagined each one would
look different depending on budget and just how big of
a name the headliners were. Was it normal to rent a
Frankenstein bus with the drummer as the driver and
pull into a near-empty campsite to spend the night
before driving the rest of the way for an evening
concert the next day?

A light streaked across the dome of the sky then

faded, bringing my gaze upward. Millions of stars sparkled against the darkness, like a seamstress had handstitched tiny sequins into the Earth's little black dress. She spun so each could catch the light and dazzle us with her beauty.

"Pretty spectacular, isn't it?" a male voice asked behind me.

My heart leapt to my throat, and I whirled on the balls of my feet. Asher stood behind me and off to the side, his hands shoved into the front pockets of his jeans and his face tipped toward the heavens.

"I can't stand under a blanket of stars like this and not feel small in comparison. It reminds me how big the universe is. How powerful and mighty God is. And yet, He loves me and knows me by name." His face lowered until he was looking at me, his features lit by the glow of our galaxy shining down on us. A small shadow fell under his cheekbone, highlighting the strong, angular cut of his jaw.

I'd heard the saying of someone having stars in their eyes before but had never paid all that much attention. Now, with constellations reflected in Asher's deep-brown irises, the saying took on a new meaning. And I couldn't look away.

"Do you see that cluster of stars over there?" His arm rose as he pointed into the distance above us. "That's Pleiades or The Seven Sisters. In Greek mythology, it's said that those stars represent the seven daughters of the Titan Atlas."

"The statue of the guy with the world on his shoulders?"

He made a humming noise in assent. "Because he was charged with carrying the heavens on his shoulders, he was gone from home and far away from his daughters for long periods of time. He was worried that the great hunter, Orion, would pursue his daughters and make them fall in love with him, so Zeus turned them into stars to comfort Atlas and so he could have his daughters closer to him." Once again, he moved his gaze from the sky to me. "Even now, the constellation of Orion is still pursuing them across the sky every night." He took a step closer.

I could feel his body heat reaching across the distance between us, invading my space but warming me in a way that I had no defense against. He pointed to the cluster of stars again, then shifted his hand a little to the side. "See him there? He's hot on their heels."

I swallowed, wondering if there was more to this little astronomy lesson than a simple jump into Greek mythology. Did he see me as Pleiades and himself as Orion? Was he trying to tell me that he'd chase after me the way Orion did Atlas's daughters?

I shifted my weight away from him, standing mostly on the foot farthest from where he stood. The cold seeped back into the space I'd created, immediately robbing me. I shivered, something that did not go unnoticed. Asher shrugged out of his jacket. I was so taken aback by the gesture (Really? Guys did this outside of movies?) that it took a moment before my brain registered his intentions. By that time, he'd settled the warm sheepskin-lined denim around my shoulders, and the earthy scent wafting up from the fabric scattered my protests before they could even form on my lips.

But I needed to. Protest, that is. A well-placed quip about how Orion should respect the seven sisters and their refusal of his advances (and maybe pick one instead of chasing after all seven of their skirts at the same time—maybe Orion was a musician as well as a great hunter). Instead, all I could do was fill my lungs with what smelled like an intoxicating mixture of earth, something chalky, and...was that rosin? Did Asher play another string instrument other than guitar?

I felt myself thawing, the outward warmth lulling me into a sense of safety that had me relaxing my vigilance, giving slow blinks instead of being wide-eyed and on alert. I pinched the inside of my elbow. The moment defenses went down, the enemy advanced. And the last thing I needed was advances from Asher.

"Both of those constellations are in the Bible, too. Did you know that?"

It took me a second to switch gears. The pinch really hadn't done all that much to infuse alertness back into me. I blamed the jacket. Usually, I was much sharper than this. Then again, had Asher really just gone from flirting to Bible quotations?

"'He who made the Pleiades and Orion, and turns deep darkness into the morning and darkens the day into night, who calls for the waters of the sea and pours them out on the surface of the earth, the Lord is his name.' Amos 5:8." He flicked his gaze at me out of the corner of his eye. "Goes back to the heavens declaring their maker, doesn't it?"

I crossed my arms and pivoted, studying him openly. I considered myself a decent judge of people, Wyatt being a huge exception. Usually, people fit pretty squarely in some sort of box. But Asher North kept trying to climb out of the box I'd put him in. Like a happy little puppy determined to knock over the cardboard confining him so he could crawl into a lap—my lap—and get attention.

"What's your deal?" I asked.

His head reared back in surprise. "My deal?"

I nodded, leaving the question broad. At that point, I'd have been happy to have any bit of him pinned down and figured out.

"I don't have a deal."

"Everyone has a deal."

He digested that for a second. "What's yours?" he asked softly.

The spotlight on me had never felt comfortable, so I clamped my teeth together.

"Tell me about your sister."

It was my turn to be surprised. "What about her?"

He shrugged. "You could always start with her name."

I didn't know why he wanted to know, but couldn't find any harm in sharing. "Her name is Bella."

Asher's growing smile did not match the info I'd just given him. Instead of a simple name, he acted like I'd let him in on some huge secret.

"Why are you impersonating the Cheshire Cat from *Alice in Wonderland?*"

"My brother's name is Aaron. Aaron, Asher— double A. Betsy, Bella—double B." Something flashed across his face, but he shuttered his thoughts faster than a door slamming in my face.

My lips turned down as my suspicions rose. A lump lodged in the pit of my stomach. I'd known it would happen. That he'd prove me right. He was just like every other guy who charmed with a guitar slung in front of him, a tune on his lips, and limelight blinding him. It had only been a matter of time. I hadn't expected this feeling of disappointment that was clammier and more weighted than humidity in Florida in August though. "You're thinking some- thing," I accused.

He tried to appear unaffected, but he didn't have near as much practice as I had with the expression and instead came off as constipated. I made myself scowl instead of letting my lips tip in any semblance of a grin.

"Of course I'm thinking something. I'm not dead."

His Adam's apple bobbed in his throat. "Besides, I have a right to private thoughts, don't I?"

"As this particular thought has to do with me, my sister, or both, then no, you don't." I propped a hand on my hip. "Tell me."

He pressed his lips together until they formed a thin line.

"Then I have no choice but to draw my own conclusions. Based off past experiences with other guys, I have to warn you, my assumptions won't be pretty."

He groaned. "Can't you judge me off my own merits?"

I pushed my lips to the side to at least give him the impression I was considering such a thing. "Not enough data collected."

"Fine." He scrubbed a hand through his hair, the ends sticking up. "The thought happened to cross my mind that AA"—he pointed to himself—"and BB"—he pointed at me—"well, that..." Two bright splotches of pink appeared in the shadows his cheekbones produced. "That if we had two kids, they could both have names that started with the letter C." He finished his sentence in a rush of words, looking anywhere but at me.

That...was not anything that I'd expected him to say. Nothing about brothers hooking up with sisters or anything else I'd been propositioned with before. But besides the content, the execution left my head spinning too. Asher exuded confidence about ninety percent of the time, but I'd never really seen him cross the line into arrogance or condescension. However, I'd been waiting for it. People always showed their true colors eventually, right? I mean, Wyatt was a perfect example. But I'd never expected Asher to get flustered or embarrassed about a confession such as that. *A* father, *B* mother, *C* child. It was sweet. Cute. I could even almost picture—

Woah! No, no, no, no.

I needed to derail that train before it had time to leave the station. There was no A+B=C. No plus sign at all. There was Asher and there was me. Separate. Opposite poles. No connection.

Then what do you call the electric charge that thinks your veins are power lines whenever he's near?

Fine. There was attraction. People were attracted to each other all the time. My younger self thought Zac Efron was hot. Did Zac Efron and I ever get together? No. No we did not. Ipso facto, alakazam, bibbidi-bobbidi-boo, Asher and I would also never be together. I mentally wiped my hands of the matter. Case closed. Door shut. End of story.

"So, you're from Argentina, huh?"

He kept spinning this conversational dime on its axis. Lucky for me, I was the merry-go-round queen of Rancho Buena Vista Elementary School. I was able to go round and round for hours without ever getting dizzy. "Yep."

My monosyllabic response didn't deter him. "The

pictures of Patagonia I've seen are breathtaking. Was it hard adjusting when you moved to the States?"

"Considering I was two, I'd say no."

He nodded like that made perfect sense. "What about for your parents?"

I shrugged. Honestly, for some reason I hadn't really considered how immigrating had affected my parents outside what I could see with my own two eyes. I'd never asked them, and they'd never said. "There's a small community of Argentines they've become a part of. My aunt and uncle and their kids currently live with us too, so they're enjoying having family close again."

He looked at me in that deep way of his. Like a surgeon with a scalpel, cutting away all the hogwash to get to the heart of the matter.

"Your sister. Your cousin. I can see that family means a lot to you."

"Family is everything," I answered without hesitating.

A sadness dimmed his features. "I envy you the closeness you have with your family."

I shouldn't ask him. Shouldn't encourage this famil-iarity he was trying to establish between us.

Opposite poles, remember?

But even though I knew I should keep my distance, I couldn't stop myself from asking. "You're not close to your family?"

He snorted in derision. "My mother's idea of closeness is a formal invitation to dine together once a month."

"Did you literally just say dine?"

His face was turned away from me, but from his profile I could see the corner of his mouth pull up in a smirk. "Cynthia North does not eat. She dines."

"Fancy schmancy."

This time he tossed a look my way. "You have no idea."

"She must be proud of you, though. Fame and fortune right at your fingertips." Yep. I heard the slight sneer in my voice.

He scoffed, ignoring my tone. "Music is not a 'real job'"—his fingers curled into air quotes—"according to her. Also, you realize all of these concerts are taking place inside churches, don't you? The NFL isn't going to be calling us anytime soon to entertain at the half-time show during the next Super Bowl. I don't know how much fame and fortune you think music ministry brings."

Huh. I hadn't considered that. Although, there were plenty of megachurches with televised pastors who were raking in the dough. But Asher was right. In regard to money, there was a lot more to be had in the mainstream market. And it wasn't like he wasn't good enough to make it amongst big names either. He could easily be topping charts and having his songs play on repeat on more than one radio station if he so chose.

"Why do you sing Christian music?"

He turned his head so he could face me straight on. "What do you mean?"

"You could sing anything. Have your name up in lights. Sell out concerts in stadiums. Have more money than you know what to do with. Why aren't you?"

He took his time answering, as if he were choosing his words carefully. "The music isn't mine," he said simply. Quietly.

"What do you mean?"

"It doesn't come from me. I'm just an instrument for God to use, kind of like my guitar. He gives me the songs, and in return I sing them for His glory."

I pursed my lips, trying to sift what he was saying and weigh it for any truth. Was he feeding me what he thought I wanted to hear, or did he truly believe everything he said?

"Careful. You're letting your cynicism show."

I schooled my face, adopting a bland expression.

"It's okay. I can tell you're not sure if you should believe me."

"It's just that…" I paused. Then paused again. Was I really stopping to consider my words and how they would make Asher feel? That didn't sound like me at all. "It's just that people like you have a knack of knowing what those around them want to hear and then saying it."

"People like me," he murmured. "You know, there really isn't a *we* or an *us*. It's just an *I* or a *me*. I know you think all musicians are the same, but that would be

similar to starting a sentence with all immigrants are…
fill in the blank. Which I'm pretty sure you wouldn't
stand for. That's the problem with generalizations,
stereotypes, and exclusions." He maintained steady eye
contact, his voice warm but lacking any burning heat.

He hooked a thumb over his shoulder. "I'm going to
go back and try to get some sleep." Without waiting for
a reply, he turned and strode back to the bus.

I pulled the collar of Asher's jacket closed at the
base of my throat, a chill working its way down my
spine. A coyote howled in the distance.

I tried to bury the thought rising in my mind, but it
clawed its way to the surface.

Could Asher be right?

14

Asher

*D*awn broke over the horizon, the early morning light bathing the distant barren hills in pastel hues of pinks and purples like an Easter egg in spring. A chill still nipped in the air, the sun not having risen enough to chase it away with its celestial broom and make room for waves of warmth to take its place. The hairs on my arms stood up, my skin pebbling against the crisp temps. Betsy still had my jacket, so I didn't have much defense against the morning air.

I pictured her as she'd looked last night, the sheepskin collar high around the back of her neck, the white wool caressing her jawline. It was such a cliché guy thing to think—that she looked good in my clothes. But she had. More than that, she'd looked...right. Natural. As if being embraced and enveloped in something of mine was how it was *supposed* to be. Maybe one day, if she ever trusted me enough to let me get close, I could be the one to fight off the cold for her as we stood under the stars. I could be the one holding her in my arms, sharing my body heat. Sharing, perhaps, even my heart.

I blew hot air into the palms of my hands and rubbed them together before I took my cell phone out of my pocket. That was the whole reason I'd left the warmth of the bus to brave the elements—to call Aaron, not reminisce about Betsy. I wanted to make sure both he and the woman he'd taken over to Mother's house the night before had survived. If I was the Cheshire Cat, as Betsy had accused under Orion's watchful gaze, then my mother was the Queen of Hearts. She'd never uttered the phrase *Off with their heads!* but she'd made plenty of heads roll in her lifetime, both in business and her personal life. Just because we were her sons did not make us safe. If anything, it placed an even bigger target on our backs.

The phone rang, and I stomped my feet to warm them up. In the distance, the sound of a zipper broke through the silence. We'd found a secluded camping site, so it was easy to forget that we weren't alone here among the rocky outcroppings. A gray hare with long ears hopped from behind a boulder, stopped, and sniffed the air, its little nose twitching.

A click emanated from the phone before my brother's voice came onto the line. "I've got ten minutes to down my second cup of coffee and an egg bite I microwaved that now tastes like rubber before I have to log in and start on my morning emails, so make it quick."

To anyone else, Aaron might sound brusque, but I smiled at the way he cut to the chase. If he'd answered the phone with a *Good morning. How are you today?* I'd know he was mad at me for some reason. He reserved that tone for clients, Mother, and anyone who'd managed to get on his bad side.

"How'd it go last night?" I asked.

"You know," he said, surprise in his voice, "pretty well, actually."

"Really? I expected it to end in tears. Yours, to be exact."

"I think you're confusing me with you, but, yeah. Tori and Mother actually seemed to hit it off."

There were things he wasn't saying. Questions behind the statements.

"Is that freaking you out?" Aaron couldn't see me, so I didn't even hide my smile, although I was sure he could hear my amusement in my tone.

"Kind of," he admitted, muffled sounds coming through in the background, like the cuffs of his sleeves rubbing his starched collar as he massaged the back of his neck. "I mean, I really like Tori. She's smart, kind, funny, and drop-dead gorgeous."

"But?"

"But..." He dropped his volume. "But I can't stop

thinking there must be something wrong with her for Mom to approve, you know?"

I hummed in response. No one but the two of us would probably understand just how impossible gaining Cynthia North's approval was. I'd given up a long time ago, although I couldn't say I didn't feel any hurt over not receiving her unconditional love. It was like having a sprained toe. You could still walk, run, do whatever you wanted to do, but not without a certain ache that you eventually learned to live with until it just became your new normal.

"And get this." He gave a disbelieving chuckle. "When we were about to head out the door, she pulled me aside and told me she was proud of me."

"Wow." I didn't think our mother even knew those words existed in the English language. "Is she dying?"

Aaron barked a laugh. "How bad is it that my first thought was exactly the same?" He sobered. "But I have to admit, it was really…" He trailed off as if he couldn't put his feelings into words. As if they were too big to be contained by twenty-six letters of the alphabet.

"That good, huh?" A twinge pinched just below my ribs.

"Yeah." A tapping sound followed, pencil against his desk. *Tap, tap, tap.* "Hey, Asher?" The edges of his voice had rounded. Softened. "I'm proud of you, man."

My eyes immediately stung. "You don't have to—"

"I'm proud of you," he interrupted. "No matter how many belittling messages you've received—from Mom, people in the industry, even me at times—you haven't let them keep you from rising above the noise. But you've done it in such a humble way, not seeking the top to prove anyone wrong, but quietly confident in your own worth and ability. You're an amazing guy, and I'm proud to call you my brother."

The lyrics of "Kumbaya" floated through my mind, and I let out a heavy breath—part frustration and part begrudging humor—that crackled in the phone.

"Too sappy?"

"What? No. Sorry. Something just came to my mind that's sort of an inside joke. But, yeah." I swallowed hard. "I'm proud to call you brother too."

"Okay." He didn't press for more details. "Well, my ten minutes are up. So unless you want me to start a timer for billable hours, I've got to go."

"Talk to you later."

We hung up, and I slid my phone back into my pocket, letting my head fall backward as I squeezed my eyes shut. Everything Aaron had said, I realized, were things I'd been yearning to hear. Maybe even for longer than I'd realized. How I hadn't let the disappointment in my own mother's eyes when she looked at me be a catalyst to prove to her my worth or seek the recognition I'd craved growing up in the shouts and accolades of fans by following after fame.

The very things Betsy had accused me of without even knowing me, I'd put intentional boundaries around because I knew how easy it would be to shift focus and try to fill holes in my life with temporal things instead of eternal. The irony would be laughable if it didn't sting so much.

But she doesn't know you, I reminded myself. And hurt people hurt people. So, really, the only thing I could do was give Betsy every opportunity to see me for me and not through the lens of her past experiences with musicians. Eventually she'd come to see that I wasn't anything like she'd already judged me to be.

A loud bang echoed in the still morning air, originating behind me. I turned and Jimmy waved, his cell pressed to his ear and his hair sticking up in all directions. Knowing him, he'd just woken up and was calling Doreen, his wife, first thing. She'd originally planned to go on tour with us—no one had liked the idea of splitting up the family—but then her mom had fallen ill, and Doreen had flown out to Florida to manage her mom's health needs.

I made a mental note to check on Jimmy and Marcus often throughout the next weeks. Tours were stressful enough on their own. Add in personal difficulties on top of that and it could potentially be a recipe for a breakdown. While we'd made commitments with each of the churches hosting us as venues, I had a greater responsibility to my bandmates and friends.

I stepped back into the bus, the smell of fresh-brewed coffee welcoming me. Someone had found a miniature coffee maker in one of the cabinets (the carafe only held two cups of near-black liquid) and had plugged it in. It took exactly one step and a pivot to enter the "kitchen" and stand in front of the leprechaun-sized Mr. Coffee. We'd need to brew at least three or four pots for everyone to have a cup. I opened an overhead cabinet in search of a mug. Best to get the second pot brewing, but I needed to empty the carafe first.

A stack of disposable to-go-style cups nestled together in the corner of the cabinet. I peeled off the top two, set them on the small square of butcher's block counter space, then grabbed the handle to remove the carafe from the maker's warming plate.

"If you value your life, you'll step away from the coffee."

I let the smile play over my lips. I'd never seen the point in schooling one's features. If I felt something—joy, anger, sadness—why should I try and hide that from other people?

Slowly, I raised my hands as if a mugger had just come up to me with a gun and threatened my life for the money in my wallet. Well, my life *had* been threatened, if unconvincingly. And yet, instead of shaking in my boots, I wanted to verbally spar with my assailant.

Keeping my palms held face out, I rotated on the balls of my feet until I faced Betsy. The smile froze on my lips as my breath exploded in my lungs. She stood a few feet away, her arms crossed over her chest and her hip cocked like a pistol ready to send a bullet to my heart. Her baggy sleep clothes were rumpled, and tiny crease marks slashed across one side of her face, left there by her pillow. Her hair looked wild, untamed, and the embodiment of the free spirit of the woman who wore it. Something about seeing Betsy like this, just out of bed first thing in the morning, felt intimate. A privilege set apart for after marriage vows.

Which struck me as strange, since I'd just seen Jimmy in a similar state and it hadn't phased me at all. The words *intimate* or *vulnerable* hadn't even considered knocking on the door of my mind. If I had to guess, the same would be true if Tricia waddled from the sleeping area and into our duet, making it a trio. No, this impression of intimacy was reserved for Betsy alone.

I cleared my throat and looked above Betsy's head to give myself a second to get a grip on my thoughts. "Is your first reaction always bodily harm?" I managed to ask around the lump in my throat.

She smirked. "You say it like it's a bad thing."

I lowered my hands and shrugged. "The saying goes that you can catch more flies with honey than vinegar."

"Why would I want even one, much less more flies?"

"I just meant a simple *please* goes a long way."

She stepped forward and gave me a shove. "So does a *get out of my way.*"

This time I was the one who folded my arms over my chest and leaned my shoulder against the door-jamb. I watched her pour the coffee into a cup and dump the contents of three sugar packets into the dark liquid.

"We had a cat once when I was growing up. My brother named it Lucifer because he said it was the devil incarnate. Lucifer would hiss and try to scratch anyone who ever tried to get close or, heaven forbid, tried to pet him. My mom threatened to take Lucifer to the pound, but I begged her not to."

Betsy stirred her coffee, pretending not to listen to my story. The slow rotation of her spoon and the tilt of her head, however, gave her away. She was more invested in the words coming out of my mouth than she wanted to let on.

"Every day I'd spend time with Lucifer. Talk to him calmly instead of yelling at him like my mom and brother did. I'd offer him treats even though he'd try to bite my fingers off for my efforts. It took time, but eventually Lucifer began to realize I didn't mean him any harm. That I wasn't scared of him, and he couldn't chase me away with his bad attitude. I'd just keep showing up with treats. Proving that I could be trusted."

She set the spoon beside her cup, then lifted the brim to her lips to take a sip, still pretending to ignore me.

"My brother thought it was funny, naming that cat Lucifer, but do you know what Lucifer means?"

I didn't expect her to answer and she didn't.

"The name means light bringer, and that cat

brought so much light into my life. For a long time, he was my best friend." I pushed off the door frame and made to walk past her, but I stopped at her back and bent until my head was next to hers. "You can hiss and scratch all you want, but you don't scare me, Betsy Vargas. One day, you'll see that I'm not going to hurt you and that you can trust me." With that, I walked to the berthing area without looking back.

15

Betsy

*W*ho did he think he was, comparing me to a cat? A cat named Lucifer, no less. Not that I'd never been called a she-devil, or even worse for that matter. But still.

The water in the tiny bathroom that was barely large enough to turn around in shut off, the pipes going quiet. In silent agreement—because, really, none of us wanted to have that pleasant conversation—we'd all decided to use the campground facilities for our toilet needs. (We'd stopped at a drive-through Mexican place for dinner the night before. Beans plus a questionable mixture of real beef and filler plus a metal cylinder of confined space did not equal a recipe any of us wanted to experience. No thank you to steeping in noxious fumes.) But this campground didn't offer showers, so it was the bus's vertical coffin or nothing.

Asher had stepped in with a towel and a folded

stack of fresh clothes ten minutes prior. I'd been tempted to slink around the exterior of the bus and find where the hook-ups were and do a little sabotaging, but I restrained myself. Let him have his hot or cold water. I'd be lukewarm. Neutral. Switzerland.

At least on the outside.

I wouldn't give him the satisfaction of seeing how his words affected me. How *he* affected me. If I didn't give him a reaction, he'd grow bored. Lose interest. Lose hope.

Which was exactly what I wanted.

A niggle of doubt tried to worm its way through my defenses. Like water seeping past cracks in a dam. Ah! I needed to prod my internal beaver to get to work and plug those holes, *rapida*. Gnaw down a tree, drag it to my resolve, and shove it inside until there was a water-tight seal that nothing could make it past.

Mutterings drifted through the walls and door, but the words were muffled enough to not be understood.

I'd become attuned to Asher. Where he was at any given time (it was a bus, after all), how he smelled (I blamed it on the jacket), and the small nuances in his facial expressions whenever there was a slight change in his mood. His eyes, for instance, dimmed when he spoke of his family. While he maintained a smile, it was a straight slash across his face. Comparatively, when-ever he talked about music, whether about the songs he was writing or a chord progression or even just talking to or about his bandmates, the left side of his mouth hooked higher up on his cheek, giving him the lopsided grin I'd noticed the first day I'd met him.

Just from the low timbre of his muffled mutterings, I could hear his exasperation. Funny. He'd never taken that tone with me, even though I'd given him plenty of opportunity to feel frustrated.

The knob on the bathroom door turned. I focused on the book in my hands, the letters all blurring together. I'd been attempting to read for the past fifteen minutes but had only managed to settle my gaze on the first paragraph three times before being over- taken by my thoughts once again. I just couldn't focus. Not on figuring out whodunit in my cozy mystery, anyway.

The door swung open and out stepped Asher.

Shirtless.

My fingers tightened on the edges of my book. It wasn't until my eyes started to sting that I realized I'd stopped blinking. I tore my gaze away from his lean form and sculpted muscles.

Way to stay unaffected, Bets.

Traitorous thrumming pulse. Disloyal shortened breaths.

He walked past where I sat on my bunk, ignoring me in my dumbfounded state. If he'd glanced over, thrown me a wink, I probably would've pounced on him faster than a leopard falling from a tree onto a gazelle. No, not like *that*. The pound of flesh I'd have taken out of his hide would've been a verbal chewing out. As it was, he didn't even seem to realize I was there. He held a wet shirt in his hands. Must've fallen on the bathroom floor and soaked up water from the shower.

He turned his back to me.

I bit the inside of my cheek. *¡Caray!* I'd never in my life considered the back a particularly attractive part of the body. Boy had I been wrong. It wasn't that Asher's shoulders were especially broad. It was more like everywhere I looked I could see definition and nuanced strength. A controlled sort of vibrancy that rippled across his skin every time he moved. An explosion of power waiting to be unleashed.

He picked up a shirt and threaded his arms through the appropriate holes. His chin turned toward me and he paused.

I pulled my book in front of my face, more to hide behind than anything else. Asher couldn't witness any of the instability swirling along in my bloodstream at that moment. He couldn't get ideas about me getting ideas. Not until I got ahold of the emergency switch and shut this baby down.

Fabric rustled, and I pictured him pulling his shirt over his head. The sound of his suitcase zipper closing came next. The carpet on the aisle muffled his footfalls, but I could still hear his steps. Then three long, slender fingers closed over the top of my book. I held my breath. He took the book out of my hands, but instead of lowering my paperback shield, he turned it upside down. Er, right side up?

Had I really been holding it wrong this entire time?

I swallowed down the growl climbing up my throat and waited for him to call me out. Say something he'd think was cutesy about how he knew he was irresistible or some other male chauvinist comment. Or something. Anything. I didn't really know what exactly, because Asher was starting to make me question everything I thought I knew about him and guys like him.

But he didn't say anything. He just continued walking toward the front of the bus.

"We need a bathroom schedule!" I shouted.

He half rotated until he was in profile.

"So Tricia and I aren't subjected to seeing you guys walking around without proper clothing." I cringed at how prudish I sounded, but I was prodding the bear more than anything. This would get him to say something about my ogling him. Accuse me of liking what I'd seen. Prove to me that my previous assessment had been right all along.

One of Asher's eyebrows rose.

I waited.

Instead of saying anything, he inclined his head. "I apologize for making you uncomfortable. There was a mishap, but I won't use that as an excuse. Of course we'll do everything we can to maintain propriety. I'll make up a sign-up sheet, and all members of the opposite gender will vacate the bus while the others shower. Does that meet with your approval?

"Umm…yes?" I jutted my chin forward. "Thank you."

When he opened the bus door and stepped outside, I flopped back onto my pillow and let out a long breath. The truth was, he *had* made me uncomfortable, but not like he'd implied. Worse. I was uncomfortable with the knowledge that my attraction to Asher wasn't dying; it was growing. I needed something that would kill the bond forming between us once and for all.

Tricia climbed into the bus, a tray of muffins in her hand. "I found a camp store near the restrooms and got us some breakfast."

Who knew Asher better than those who'd spent the most time with him—his bandmates? They'd be able to tell me who he really was, how he really acted when he wasn't trying to impress or win someone over. They probably had all sorts of dirt on him they could share. Once I knew all of that, I'd stop second-guessing myself and recement why I'd made a rule about falling for musicians in the first place.

Tricia found a roll of paper towels and ripped off a rectangle on the perforated edge. She set a muffin on top of the paper and held it out to me. "Muffin?"

I accepted with a thanks. "Hey, Trish. Can I ask you a question?"

She peeled the muffin liner away from the sides of her baked good. "Sure. What's up?"

"How long have you known Asher?"

She chewed slowly, considering. "About three years or so. Why?"

I shrugged, trying to appear nonchalant. "No reason." I took a bite and forced myself not to gag at the smushed banana flavor. I put the muffin to the side to keep myself from forgetting and taking another bite. "Just trying to get to know the boss man better, I guess."

"Oh, he'd hate to hear you call him that."

"Call him what?"

"The boss."

I tilted my head. "Why?"

"Asher doesn't consider himself the boss."

"Even though the band bears his name and he's the lead singer and guitarist?"

She nodded as she chewed. "The name True North was actually Jimmy's wife's idea. She thought it was a clever play on Asher's name but also a reminder to our audience to look toward the One who is our own personal true north and director of our paths—Jesus." Crumbs fell from her lips to land on top of her rounded belly. She brushed them into a neat pile. "Asher tried to argue, but we all liked the name and the meaning behind it, so he got outvoted and we kept it." Tricia pinched the crumbs in her fingers and deposited them into the paper muffin liner.

"So, he didn't want his name as a headliner?" The

incredulity in my voice gave away my interest, and I tried to rein the physical display in.

Tricia folded the liner in half then in half again. "Nope. I think it embarrassed him a lot at first. As much as he loves to share music with others, I don't think he enjoys the spotlight as much as some other people I've come across. More like he endures it as part of his job and because he feels like ministering through music is something he's been called to do."

"Huh." That was not what I'd expected her to say.

"What about you?" She folded her hands primly and looked at me with undivided attention. "Asher has said you're in possession of a singing voice unlike he's ever heard before."

I trailed the pattern of the fabricated wall with my gaze. Somehow, I'd let the conversation turn away from unearthing dirt on Asher to digging into my own life. "He exaggerates."

Tricia snorted. "Not likely. I've never heard him say anything he didn't truly mean." She leaned forward. "I know he's hoping you'll eventually find your way on stage with us."

My bones turned to ice even though we were in the desert. I knew of Asher's pipe dream, but even the idea of getting on stage made me nauseous. It wasn't the fear of failure or of the stage or the lights or the audience that made me determined never to step foot on the raised platform. It was fear of success. If I lost my head to the adrenaline and endorphin rush of performing as much as I'd already lost my heart to music itself, what would keep me from becoming just like the people I despised?

"I have to run the soundboard." That's what I'd been hired to do. My job.

Tricia tossed her hand in the air, batting away my reasoning like a cat with a ball of yarn. "All the places we're scheduled to play are large churches with their own PA systems and knowledgeable people who run the equipment every weekend. You could easily walk away for a set or two and we'd all be fine and still sound great."

"I…" really didn't know how to respond to that. Had Asher—

Tricia hissed in a sharp breath through her teeth. She curled around her middle—as much as one could curl around a watermelon.

I put a tentative hand on her shoulder. "Are you okay? Should I get someone?"

Her eyes squeezed shut but she shook her head. After a moment, her eyes opened and her cheeks puffed out as she huffed. "Braxton Hicks."

Should've known. Bella had experienced something similar, although not until about a week before Charlotte was born. "I know you're tired of hearing this, but are you sure living on a bus and performing every night is really the best idea for you right now?"

She reached behind herself and tried to massage her lower back with her fingertips. I made a turn motion by spinning my index finger in the air, and she obeyed. I pressed my thumbs into the muscles along her spine.

She moaned. "That feels so good. Thank you. Also, you sound just like Asher. He's been trying to tell me he'd postpone this tour ever since he found out I was pregnant, even though doing so could be a detriment to his career."

"What do you mean?" I pushed small circles into her aching back to work out the tight muscles.

"There's a representative from a record label that's going to come out to hear us when we play in Los Angeles."

My hands stilled. "Wow. That could be huge for all of you."

Tricia was shaking her head even before I'd finished my sentence. "I plan on staying home to raise this baby once she's born." She caressed the side of her stomach. "Jimmy and Marcus started playing for the worship team during church services. Marcus had begun to get into some trouble, and Jimmy was desperately searching for an avenue to reach his son. That's how they met Asher. The band is more of a hobby they can do together. Neither one of them wants to make this gig into a lifetime career. Jimmy works from home, which is how he can get away for this tour, but Marcus is headed to college next year. Besides Asher, Dave's the only one who considers music a viable occupation option."

I absorbed this information. "Let me get this

straight. Asher knows the label will be at the concert and what that means for him personally, but he tried to cancel anyway?"

Tricia nodded, happy to see I was finally catching on. "For me, because of the pregnancy, and for Marcus, because he needs to study for college entrance exams and get his applications in order and sent out."

"But why would he do that if he knows this is his chance to break through and make a name for himself?" It didn't make sense.

Wyatt had dropped Bella at the first whiff of an opportunity, and his shot hadn't even been as big as someone from a label seeing him live. Even Malachi's brother, who I could admit was a descent sort of fellow, if misguided, (at least he had eventually come to his senses, unlike some others blinded by ambition) had gotten himself into debt and risked his family legacy for just a chance at something big.

Tricia patted the back of my hand. "I told you, Asher doesn't care about a bunch of people knowing his name, winning awards, or any of that sort of thing. But his reason? First Corinthians chapter thirteen lists a lot of things love is and isn't—one of those things being love is not self-seeking. Simple as that."

A tug-of-war started up in my insides. Asher North was turning out to be anything but simple.

16

Asher

The drive into the Las Vegas area had been quieter than I'd expected. Well, as quiet as a Frankenstein bus could be. The vehicle shook, rattled, and rolled more than Bill Haley and his Comets on the *Ed Sullivan Show* back in the fifties. Other than the moaning and groaning from Igor, however, everyone else had been relatively mute.

Jimmy had stated he hadn't slept well the night before so was passed out on the bunk, Marcus sprawled in the bed under him studying from a biology textbook. Tricia sat in the banquette with her chin propped into the palm of her hand as she looked out the window and watched the scenery pass by, while Dave drove and Betsy pretended to read her book.

I covered my mouth with my hand to hide my smile. I never would have thought it possible to render Betsy speechless. She had the quickest comebacks and razor-sharp comments of anyone I'd ever met. Her wit might have scared me if I didn't find it so completely attractive. Nor had I thought I'd ever catch her hiding —from anything, but especially not from me. She was the type of person who didn't back down. Who was ready to fight and stand her ground instead of tucking tail and running.

Honestly, I'd found myself wondering what it would be like with Betsy and Mother in the same room. Cynthia North could make any human with a beating heart cower, but I somehow suspected Betsy wouldn't kowtow. She'd give as good as she got and maybe even come out the victor. Because Mother's dining room would probably turn into a verbal boxing ring if I ever brought Betsy there to meet my family.

I mentally grabbed the trailing leash of my thoughts and pulled them back like a puppy needing to learn to heel. The point wasn't that I'd allowed myself to wonder what would happen if I introduced Betsy to my mother. The point was that Betsy had become tongue-tied and had even tried to back away and make herself unseen. Because of me.

I tried to keep my chest from inflating too much. I wasn't successful, but it was the trying that counted, right? I wouldn't have been lying if I'd said I'd come out of the bathroom without a shirt on against my will. I'd planned to be fully clothed. But then my elbow had knocked my tee off the miniscule sink into the sudsy puddle, and the cotton had become soaked. I hadn't had any other option but to retrieve a new shirt, and to do that, I'd had to leave the privacy of the bathroom shirtless. The whole thing had been innocent and unintentional.

If I'd said I hadn't been pleased with the reaction I'd gotten from Betsy, now *that* would have been lying. Ever since I'd met her, she'd kept her expressions bland and blasé. I never knew what she was truly thinking or feeling. Even if she did say something, I'd wonder if her sarcasm was really a smokescreen, so I'd wait for the effects of her flash-bang to dissipate, then peer deeper.

But today that had been stripped away. What I'd seen on her face for one unguarded second had been raw, vulnerable, and had set my soul on fire. She'd quickly reset her walls and tried to prod me to a reaction, but no matter how many redirects she'd thrown at me, I'd never forget the slackness of her jaw, the flush of her skin, or the proof in her eyes that this pull I felt between us wasn't one sided. She felt it too.

"I think this is our exit coming up." Dave pointed out the windshield to the green road signs above the highway. He hated the computerized voices on phone GPS systems so had made anyone occupying the passenger seat the navigator.

I looked down at the muted phone in my hands. The directions did say to exit. "Yeah, you're going to get off here and go another ten miles."

Large shadows covered portions of the wide blanket of barren land, cast by white cotton ball-type clouds floating in the sea of blue above. We'd miss driving into the heart of the iconic city, although the black pyramid of the Luxor Hotel and Casino as well as the skylines of the MGM Grand and the Eiffel Tower's doppelganger at the Paris Las Vegas Hotel were hard to miss. Since the city never slept, we could always head to the strip after the concert and see the Bellagio fountains or pretend we were in Venice and go on a gondola ride at the Venetian. Then again, once the final notes were played, the audience went home, and we packed all the equipment back up, the only thing any of us would want to do was crash.

Dave pulled into a church that hadn't quite grown into the title of *mega* yet. The building occupancy had been set at eight hundred people. Instead of selling tickets, the church had hired us outright for their congregants and as a community outreach opportunity. Drought-resistant plants sprawled across the grounds, popping up between beds of gleaming white rocks, while the building itself had a sloping roof on either side from a central three-story metal cross. The whole effect was grand and impressive.

Dave killed the engine, and we all exited the bus, our eyes pulled skyward by the massive cross. Clicking heels dragged my gaze back downward. A smartly dressed middle-aged woman made a beeline toward us from the glass door entrance.

"Welcome to Connect Church." Her arm swept to the side. "My name is Mona, and let me just say on behalf of everyone that we are so pleased to have you with us."

Tricia was closest and reached out her hand to shake Mona's. "We're thrilled to be here."

Mona beamed. "Why don't I show you all around a little bit, and then you can start setting up or do whatever you need to do."

We followed Mona inside, the lobby making us crane our necks again to peer up at the height of the ceilings. The whole front wall was made of glass, letting in natural light, the vertical beam of the cross in the middle of where two glass panels met. Stairs rounded from both sides and merged in a Juliette balcony with doors on the other far wall for second-floor seating.

Mona led us down a hallway in the right wing, then stopped at a door. "A few of the children's rooms have been made available for you to get ready in or for wardrobe changes or whatever you need." She pushed open the door and stepped aside so we could enter.

A rainbow area rug lay on top of the thin wall-to-wall commercial carpet, a semi-circle of munchkin-sized chairs around that. There was a woven basket holding tambourines by an upright piano. One wall had been painted in an animal-themed mural while the rest held brightly colored posters with inspirational sayings and Bible verses in fancy fonts.

Besides having to fold my body onto a half-sized chair if I wanted to sit, the room worked. We didn't have wardrobe changes. We weren't doing a live show to entertain with multiple costumes, choreographed dances, smoke machines, pyrotechnics, or any of that type of stuff. Not that there was anything wrong with a single one of those things—they just weren't who we were. Our songs weren't about entertainment so much as they were edification and glorification of our audience of One.

Mona showed us a similar room that she said was for the women in our group. Next, she led us to a door near the back. It opened up to a vestibule, the stage visible from the side.

"If you want to get a feel for the platform, go right ahead." Mona gestured for us to exit the wings and walk onto the podium.

Dave and Jimmy passed me, their feet taking them forward while their necks craned around so they could absorb the experience from every angle all at once. Tricia silently mouthed *wow* as her eyes widened. Even from my vantage point I could see the sanctuary resembled more of an auditorium. Up until now, we'd played mostly for local churches of varying sizes. This was by far the biggest venue we'd ever performed in.

Betsy stood beside me in the vestibule. I looked down at her. "Coming?"

She stubbornly shook her head. "I'm good right here."

"You know you're going to walk on that stage eventually." I gave her a good-natured nudge with my elbow.

Her eyes flashed, and she poked me in the chest. "Listen here, Asher North. I am—"

"To set up the sound equipment," I interrupted with my lips tingling. I wanted to grin but instead adopted an innocent look. "What did you think I meant?"

She scowled but didn't answer. Instead, she marched onto the shining pine platform. I followed, my silent chuckles rumbling in my chest. Her foot suddenly skated away from her like a cute little rebellious penguin on the ice, and she pitched forward. In one swift move, I was at her side and cupping her elbow, lending her my strength to steady herself.

Her chin lifted at the same time I tilted mine down. At this proximity and this angle, our lips were only a breath apart. I meant to ask if she was okay, but the words lodged in the lump in my throat. Her veil of indifference slipped, and her gaze darted down to my mouth. I stood completely still, not even daring to breathe. I willed her to see me for me and not through the lens of her prejudice. To see that I could be trusted. That something between us could be beautiful if she'd only let herself be open to the possibility.

I'd promised myself I'd be patient. That I'd prove myself to Betsy. So, one by one, I reluctantly peeled my fingers away from her skin and dropped my hand. I took a step away from her. Then another, my eyes locked on hers, hoping she'd see the promise in them.

When I made to pivot, my foot slid out from under me, the floor as slick as a freshly greased pig. My arms windmilled, but my fingers only grasped the air. Gravity reached out and snatched me, cackling with laughter as I fell like a redwood in the forest, landing on my side.

My eyes squeezed shut as pain radiated from my elbow. I lay on my back and waited for the sharp edges to dull.

"Are you dead, man?" Dave's horrible Jamaican accent came from above me. Last year, right before the winter Olympics, we'd watched *Cool Runnings* starring John Candy and Doug E. Doug to celebrate the fact Jamaica had another bobsled team competing after thirty-four years.

"Yeah, man." I did my best Sanka impression, but my accent was just as bad as Dave's.

I blinked open my eyes, and a ring of faces stared down at me. Tricia looked genuinely concerned while the trio of guys appeared to be barely containing their laughter. Betsy...well, Betsy was shaking her head and clucking her tongue, her lips dramatically pushed out in a condescending pout.

"*Pobrecito*," she cooed as if consoling a child who'd just gotten a boo-boo.

I planted my palm on the floor to push myself up into a sitting position, but my fingers started to slide apart into the splits. Good grief. Whoever had waxed and polished the wood had been a little too generous, making the stage as slippery as a Malibu sunbather slathered in tanning lotion.

I managed to get myself upright and took inventory. My hip ached but not too bad. My elbow still smarted though. I rotated my arm to try and get a look, but the position was awkward, to say the least.

The other band members drifted away, talking about instrument placement and the acoustics in the room.

Betsy squatted beside me. "Let me see." Her fingers encircled my forearm, and she gently pulled to get a better view. The curtain of her spiral curls fell to cover the side of her face. She made a noise in the back of her throat, then took her fingertips and rubbed my elbow where it hurt in a circular motion.

"Sana, sana, colita de rana. Sí no sana hoy, sanarás mañana." Finally, she gave my elbow a quick, painless smack, then sat back on her heels as if she'd just made everything better.

I wasn't going to take the time to examine the how and why of no longer feeling any pain. "What was that?"

She pushed her hair away from her face and tucked the thick mass behind her ears. "What was what?"

"What you just said. What did it mean?"

Her lips tipped up in a tease of a smile. "The meaning kind of gets lost in translation. It doesn't really make sense in English."

I moved my legs to sit crisscross. "I'd still like to hear."

She rolled her eyes. "Fine, but I warned you. Literally translated, I said, 'Heal, heal, little tail of the frog. If you don't heal today, you'll heal tomorrow.'"

I twisted my arm to look at my elbow again. "The elbow is a frog's tail in Spanish?"

"No. Elbow in Spanish is *el codo*. The rhyme is something parents in some Latin American countries say to their kids to make them feel better when they've hurt themselves. Kinda like parents here in the United States kiss their kid's boo-boos to make them feel better. It wouldn't matter if you hurt your elbow or your shin, the saying is the same."

I bent my arm at the elbow joint, back and forth. "You should patent that. It really works."

She huffed a *duh*. "Of course it works."

I leaned back, supporting my weight on my palms, then readjusted when my hands started to do a slow slide away from me. "Any other secret saying or remarkable traditions I should be aware of? I feel like I've been missing out."

She rolled her lips between her teeth, considering. With an imperceptible lift of her shoulders, she leaned toward me ever so slightly. "These aren't secrets, as every Hispanic abuela has passed on these little facts, so I guess it would be okay to let you in on them as well." She smirked. "Not your fault you didn't have the privilege of an abuela to teach you in the first place."

"No, it's not." I matched her posture. "I'm listening."

"First, never sweep a single woman's feet or let your feet get swept."

"Like, with a broom?"

"Of course with a broom. You use something else to sweep the floor besides a broom?" She tsked. "And stop smiling, *payaso*."

I grinned wider. "So why is getting one's feet swept bad?"

"The person who gets their feet swept will never get married," she said matter-of-factly.

My brows rose. "Seriously?"

"It may sound ridiculous to you, but we don't question these things. They just are."

I nodded. "Okay, what else?"

"If your left palm itches, you'll be losing money in the near future. You can try to combat that by scratching your left palm away from your body and keeping your hand open, but that might not work. However, if it's your right hand that itches, that means you are going to receive money soon. Some say to not scratch so you don't jinx your luck, but my abuela said to scratch toward your body, make a fist, then put that fist in your pocket just like you'll put the money in your pocket."

"Is that what you do?"

"Of course. If she's right, I don't want to miss the opportunity for a payday."

"Makes sense." Every culture had their superstitions. Interesting, sure, but even more than that, Betsy was opening up and sharing something personal with me. Things about her heritage and how she'd been raised. Things that were important to her, and traditions she held dear. That were a part of who she was at her core.

"What else?" I placed my elbows on my knees, eager to learn more. I was the student, and while Betsy was the teacher, she was also the subject matter. One day, I'd ace this test.

Her head tilted to the side as she thought. "Eat twelve grapes before midnight on New Year's Eve. For every grape, you make a wish. One grape and one wish for each month of the year."

"I have a cousin who lives in Georgia that says you have to eat black-eyed peas on New Year's to bring luck and good fortune for that year. I think I'd rather eat the grapes."

"You guys ready to keep going?" Jimmy called from the bottom of the platform.

I stood and held out my hand to help Betsy up. To my surprise, she slid her fingers across mine and allowed me to pull her to standing. I gave a gentle squeeze before letting go.

"Careful of your step," she warned as she shuffled her way to the risers to descend off the stage. "I brought some anti-slip tape that we can put on the bottom of everyone's shoes so we don't have any mishaps this evening. The last thing we want is for

Dave to slide headfirst into his drums or you to reenact a stooge on a banana peel and fall on your guitar."

"Well, aren't you Little Miss Prepared for Anything," I said, impressed. I'd have never thought to pack something like that. Wouldn't even cross my mind in a million years.

"I try to be." She got a funny look on her face as she turned away. "And yet I keep finding myself not prepared at all," she said as if to herself.

She wasn't talking about the concerts or what might arise because of the performances.

She was talking about me.

Betsy

"Hey, Jimmy." I reached out a hand and caught the keyboardist's arm as he made to pass me in the hall. "Can I talk to you for a minute?"

"Sure. What's up?"

I looked up and down the hall. No one else was around, but I didn't want our conversation to be overheard. Not that I felt guilty or thought I was doing anything wrong, just…I didn't want Asher to know I was asking about him.

I felt behind me, and my fingers connected with a door knob. Twisting the handle, I opened the door and took a step backward into the room, motioning for Jimmy to follow me with a flick of my head.

His forehead creased more than the khaki pants he was wearing, but he stepped into the children's room that had been designated for Tricia's and my use.

"Something wrong?" he asked.

"No, no, everything is fine," I assured him. "I just had some questions. About Asher."

The horizontal lines running between his eyebrows and hairline deepened. "What about him?"

I shrugged and arranged my face into my normal, nonchalant, couldn't-care-less expression. "Where did you two meet?"

"At church. He's been working with the praise team there for years."

I nodded like this was new information. "How did the band come together?"

Jimmy let out a single punctuation of laughter as he relaxed into a smile. "I don't know. We were talking one day after services. I was sharing with him some struggles my wife and I were having with Marcus, and he asked if Marcus was interested in music at all." Jimmy casually hooked his thumbs in his belt loops. "Marcus wasn't really interested in anything at the time. Or if he was, he never shared it with Doreen or me. Anyway, Asher came to the house the next day and challenged Marcus to a competition on Guitar Hero—you know, the video game? They were in the basement playing for hours. I don't know what Asher said to Marcus, but he came back the next day with a bass guitar and taught my son how to play. I dusted off my keyboard, and everything else sort of just fell into place after that."

I nodded some more. *¡Caray!* Just call me a bobble-head. "That seems very…magnanimous of Asher."

"He's a generous person."

I made a humming noise, neither agreeing nor disagreeing. "Not entirely altruistic on his part though, right? I mean, it's you and Marcus who've had to make the sacrifices to be here. Away from your wife. Time off of work. Marcus juggling school responsibilities and commitments while figuring out his future."

Jimmy's eyes narrowed. His steady gaze made me want to squirm away, but I held myself still.

"I see what you're doing," he said, bemusement smoothing out the lines around his mouth.

I cocked my hip. "And what do you think I'm doing besides asking a few simple questions?"

"You're looking for excuses."

The way he laid the accusation at my feet spoke of assurance. There wasn't a shadow of a doubt in his mind that he'd nailed my motivation on the head.

I lifted my chin. "An excuse for what, might I ask?"

"To keep fighting the chemistry between you and Asher."

I sputtered, denial salty on my lips.

"You can say I'm wrong, but anyone with eyes who observes the two of you for half a second can see it. Scratch that. They don't even have to see it. They can feel the electric charge in the air when you guys are in the same vicinity." He stopped and considered me again. "Why are you scared?"

I scoffed, a rebuttal of words pouring down from my brain to my mouth in a waterfall to drown Jimmy in, but before I could form even one, he held up a palm.

"Never mind. I can see you're not ready to face your feelings yet." He turned to go, stopping after opening the door rather than walking through it. "Asher is a really great guy. If you can't see that or don't *want* to see it for whatever reason, then…" He shook his head and walked away.

I blinked at the empty doorway, my fingers tingling and a ringing in my ears. Black and white had mixed together to form gray, and I couldn't seem to separate them anymore. Things had been easier, less confusing, when I'd been able to put Asher in a box and close the lid on him. Stick a label on him, give myself a rule, and keep my distance.

But he kept erasing the boundaries I'd set. Relabeling himself. He was a musician, but he didn't only think about himself—he put others first. He performed in front of audiences, but he didn't seek fame above all else. He had talent and gifts but still managed to stay humble and self-effacing.

I let my head fall forward, the muscles in the back of my neck pulling taut. Most of my life, I'd been aware of prejudices, of stereotypes. They weren't always directed straight at me, because my skin was lighter and I spoke without an accent. But I heard what people said. Immigrants were criminals. Immigrants took away jobs and hurt the economy. We were lazy or dirty or any other number of hurtful adjectives. All because of bias, rhetoric, and misinformation.

But what had I done? I'd turned around and done the same thing. Not to a race or a culture, but to Asher. To everyone who wanted to make music a career. I was guilty of the very thing I hated, and I owed him an apology.

Dave walked the hall and came to an abrupt halt in the middle of the doorway. "There you are. We're ready for the sound check."

"Coming." I followed him out to the hall and shut the door behind me.

We'd already set up the instruments and equipment earlier in the day but had taken a break. I needed to make sure everything sounded perfect with each section and then all together as a whole.

We entered the side vestibule where my sound-board had been unpacked and assembled. Dave continued on to the stage while I stopped at what essentially was my own instrument of knobs, dials, and connections. My gaze snagged on a to-go cup of coffee sitting beside what looked to be a folded shirt.

My first reaction was annoyance. Who thought leaving spillable liquid by electronic equipment was a good idea? I moved the still-warm cup to the floor, where it couldn't potentially cause a lot of damage. I went to move the shirt as well but didn't get my hand under all the layers, and it unfolded, the hem falling toward the floor. A laugh bubbled its way up my chest.

Beneath the crew neckline it read, *I run on coffee, sarcasm, and Jesus.*

How perfectly fitting for me.

I looked up, my gaze colliding with Asher's. He had his guitar strap slung over his shoulder and the instrument poised in front of him. He gave me a two-finger salute along with his lopsided grin.

And I swayed.

Me. Grumpy, impenetrable, hard-as-a-rock Betsy Vargas, swayed toward Asher North, guitarist and lead singer. I could fool myself. Say it was only the trick of gravity or a momentary feeling of unbalance, but that would just be me still looking for excuses like Jimmy accused.

Was I ready to admit the truth, though? That Asher had slowly been pulling me toward him since the moment we met, like the moon coaxing the tide higher onto the shore?

I cleared my throat and turned on the console, processor, speakers, then monitors. After a few quick checks for each speaker and monitor, I sent the mic signal to the stage right wedge and turned up the gain until it started to feedback, then identified the offending frequency and attenuated it until the feedback stopped. When all the wedges were rung out, I tuned the room by putting on a mixed song I'd made that represented all the frequency ranges, then focusing on how it sounded in the Connect Church sanctuary and on this system. A few adjustments on the EQ and everything sounded right.

I brought the fader to unity. "Okay, Dave. Give me some beats on your kick."

We went through each of Dave's channels—kick, snare, toms, cymbal mics, and overheads, then moved on to Marcus on bass, Asher's guitar, Jimmy on keyboard, then finally Tricia's mic and Asher's, checking gain, fader, gate, EQ, compression, and FX sends.

"Let's run through a song to see how you sound all together."

I made some adjustments—mostly unburying the vocals—before I was satisfied and finally gave a thumbs-up. True North was ready for their first big show, which would start in—I glanced at my wrist-watch—less than an hour.

The guys headed to their room while I followed Tricia to ours, the coffee cup held in one hand and the shirt slung over that same arm. I helped Tricia curl her hair and changed into the tee Asher had left me. My signature look—snarky T-shirt and faded jeans. For some reason, the shirt made me feel warm. Not hot and sticky like during summer heat, but cozy and contented, like a comforting spread of affection from the inside out.

It was just a shirt—some cotton-blend material with a few words screen-printed on it—so I shouldn't have been feeling like there was something overflowing inside of me. Like I had a cup somewhere in the middle of my chest that, unbeknownst to me, Asher had been sneaking to and slowly filling up by pouring himself into it until it had finally become so full it spilled over.

Just a shirt. But instead of saying *I run on coffee, sarcasm, and Jesus*, it said, *I see you, Betsy, and I like what I see. I don't want to change you even a little.*

My nose stung, and I sniffed back emotion. My family loved me. My sewing sisters loved me. But even they made comments.

"*You should smile more, Betsy.*"

"*Maybe tone down the snark.*"

"*Don't be so prickly all the time.*"

Could Asher really like even those parts of my personality?

Tricia opened the door. "It's time," she said.

I gave her a wobbly smile and followed her back to the vestibule beside the stage. The guys were already there. Marcus was opening and closing his fists while Jimmy rotated his shoulders in a circular motion. Asher stared off into space, and Dave kept muttering something to himself under his breath. Every single one of them was keyed up on nervous energy and jittering in their own way.

The sanctuary acoustics absorbed the chatter and noise of people taking their seats and waiting for the concert to start, then spat those sounds right back out into the space.

Mona walked into the wing with a gentleman knocking on the door of fifty and wearing a pair of fitted jeans and casual button-up with the top button undone. "This is Pastor David," she introduced.

He made the rounds of shaking each hand. "So glad you guys could be here tonight. We ready to get the show started?"

Heads bobbed, which made Pastor David smile wider. "All right, then. I'll go out and introduce you, then it's all yours."

The crowd began to hush as the pastor walked out of the wing onto the stage. He stopped in front of Asher's mic, gave a short intro for the band, then led the audience in a welcoming round of applause.

"This is it," Dave said at the same time Marcus muttered, "I think I'm going to be sick."

Asher turned to face them, his back to the waiting crowd. "We're really only playing for an audience of One, right?"

Marcus still looked green but answered, "Right," with everyone else.

Asher gave them all an encouraging smile, then led them onto the stage. He took his place near the center and beamed into the audience. "Hello, Las Vegas!"

I focused more on the sound than his words, and in a few moments, Dave was counting down the beat and the opening set started.

My phone buzzed in my back pocket. I adjusted an EQ. It buzzed again. And again. Jimmy played a refrain.

More buzzing. Who was blowing up my phone? I whipped it out of my pocket, the screen lighting up to show I had ten missed text messages. I was tempted to see, to make sure there hadn't been an emergency, but instead, I powered off my phone. I needed to focus. To do a good job for Asher and the band.

Asher's voice, rich and mellow, beckoned to me. He sang, and everything else faded away. The quality of his tone was hypnotizing, putting me under some sort of spell—the magic of a snake charmer, with me the cobra under the trance he'd put me in. He had that *thing*. That unexplainable, couldn't-quite-put-your-finger-on-it quality. Star power. And I somehow, against my will, had been pulled into his orbit.

The concert progressed with only a few hiccups. I was able to adjust so that I didn't think anyone in the seats could tell. Overall, the band sounded great. They'd done an amazing job, and the crowd loved them. Asher may not have been the type of person to crave recognition, but I knew music. It wouldn't take long before millions of people knew his name. Especially not with the rep from the label coming to hear him.

The band wrapped up its last song, and everyone came to their feet in a roar of applause. Asher thanked them, embarrassment tingeing his cheeks and humility in the duck of his head. His sincerity only seemed to make them love him more. My heart swelled.

Stop that. But I wasn't sure I even meant it. Asher

wasn't who I'd thought he'd be. Hadn't he proven that over and over? He was true and honorable. Loyal, with a kind heart. So what was stopping me from admitting that I'd developed feelings for an American who poured out his heart and his soul for everyone to see and hear in his music? My own stupid rule? Logic dictated, if I made the rule, then I could break it. Besides, I wasn't exactly known for following every letter of the law to a tee anyway.

Energy pulsed from Asher as he strode from the stage toward my little area. His eyes were so bright he nearly glowed. I stepped out from behind the sound-board ready to hand out some well-deserved *good jobs* to all of them—even Dave, who'd managed to push beyond robotic mechanics on his drums and actually feel the beat at the nucleus of his being.

Asher barreled forward, pushed by the high he rode from the music lifting him to elevated levels he'd prob-ably never experienced before. Instead of stopping in front of me, he swallowed up the distance and devoured my personal space, wrapping his slightly sweaty arms around my body and pulling me hard into his chest. He lifted me off my feet, and for a moment I was weightless. In more ways than just the physical sense. He laughed, and I felt his warm breath against my ear, the rumble in his chest vibrating against my entire body. He was joy, and it spilled over, filling that internal cup I hadn't even known I possessed until it overflowed into a puddle.

I was a puddle.

As if coming to his senses, he set me on my feet, the band of his arms slowly loosening from around me. He leaned back. Looked down into my eyes. His pupils dilated, and his Adam's apple bobbed.

My gaze dipped to his lips. They glistened as if he'd recently licked them. What would they feel like? Taste like? Would I hear the sounds of a string quartet or the overwhelming pounding of my heart in my ears like a Japanese taiko drum?

"We should talk," he said, the movement of his lips mesmerizing me.

I managed to pull my gaze away and lift my eyes back to his.

There was a juxtaposition of opposites there. Both tightly held control waiting to be released and relaxed confidence. Serious intent and playful mirth. A promise of things to come, and a forfeit of the present.

"After." He took a small step back and put his hands on my shoulders. Squeezed. "I have to go mingle. Try to sell some CDs and other merch. But after. I'll find you and we'll talk. Okay?"

I nodded, and he looked like he wanted to pull me into another hug but stopped himself. I congratulated Tricia, Dave, Jimmy, and Marcus, then they, too, went to the lobby to grab refreshments, mingle, and man the table they'd set up to sell their music.

Considering how people-y the lobby was, I sat back in my chair. I'd rather hide with my soundboard than make small talk with a bunch of strangers I didn't care about. Instead, I powered my phone back on, saying a silent prayer that I wasn't about to read bad news. I unlocked the screen and opened the text message app. Not an emergency from my family. A group text from the girls. I clicked on the unread thread and scrolled to the top to read from the beginning.

Jocelyn: Guess what?!?!

Molly: WHAT!!!

Jocelyn: *A picture of an engagement ring on her finger* Malachi proposed! I'm getting married!

Finally, I said in my mind even as I smiled. Jocelyn and Malachi getting married had never been a matter of *if* but *when*.

Nicole: Congratulations!

Amanda: Tell us everything!

Jocelyn: Well, he told me to meet him on top of the Empire State Building.

Amanda: Like in *Sleepless in Seattle*?

Nicole: Like in *An Affair to Remember*?

Molly: As long as it wasn't like in *King Kong*.

I rolled my eyes as I chuckled. Leave it to Molly.

Jocelyn: Do you want the story or not?

Amanda: We want!

Jocelyn: So he asked me to meet him and I didn't really think anything of it. I've been super swamped here in NY getting everything settled, so we haven't had time to do any sight-seeing so I thought that's what it was. But when I got to the top, there were flowers everywhere and Malachi stood in the middle of them all dressed in a suit. As soon as I stepped out of the elevator, he got down on one knee and asked me to be his wife.

Molly: You can't hear me, but I'm screaming.

Nicole: That's the sweetest thing ever.

Jocelyn: I'm so happy. I love him so much.

Amanda: When's the wedding?

Jocelyn: Don't worry. We won't encroach on either your or Nicole's big day.

Amanda: You know I wasn't worried about that.

Jocelyn: We'll probably just have a small ceremony at the ranch. Family and super close friends only.

Molly: Are you going to ride up on Domino? *horse emoji*

Jocelyn: Oh! I hadn't even thought of that.

Nicole: I'm so happy for you guys.

Amanda: Now all we need is for Betsy to fall in love and get engaged and we all can live happily ever after.

Nicole: You do realize a woman can live happily ever after without a man, right?

Molly: Says the woman two months out from her wedding day.

Nicole: Jocelyn, when you get back, we need to celebrate.

Jocelyn: Malachi's grandma is already planning a party. You all are invited, of course. It's short notice, next week actually. So if you can't make it, I understand.

Molly: Ben, Chloe, and I will be there.

Nicole: Sierra, Drew, and me as well.

Amanda: Count Peter and me as RSVPed.

Jocelyn: Betsy, I know you're on tour, so don't feel bad. I still love your cranky self.

Molly: Love you, Bets!

Amanda: *heart emoji*

I tapped on the screen to bring the keyboard up and thumbed out a reply.

Betsy: Congratulations, Jocelyn! I'm so happy for you and Malachi. I'll see what I can do about the party. Will have to check what location we're in at that time. Amanda, you'll be happy to know I'm reconsidering my rule. Maybe not all musicians are bad. Some of them might even be worth getting to know better. *winky face emoji*

18

Asher

My smile had been pinned in place with tape, superglue, and tacks. Anything to keep my lips from slipping from their bowed position on my face, my gritted teeth the only thing keeping my thoughts in my head and not rushing out on a wave of impatience. I was grateful. I was. The night had gone better than I could've ever hoped or asked for. The audience had been engaged during the concert, and we'd sold more merchandize than I'd ever dreamed. But instead of basking in that, all I could see was the look on Betsy's face when I'd come off the stage. I hadn't planned on hugging her, on literally sweeping her off her feet. But I'd been floating on a sea of endorphins and had let the current take me right past my self-control.

Then I'd set her on her feet and stepped back. It was like all the air had been sucked out of the room. Tricia and Jimmy had commented earlier in the night that Betsy had been asking about me, but I hadn't taken the time to consider it much. Hadn't allowed myself to wonder so I wouldn't jump the gun. The plan was proof through patience, after all. But the unshuttered look she'd given me as I'd stared down at her face had made me want to dive into the deep end then and there.

Her inspection of my lips hadn't gone unnoticed, and I'd read her thoughts easily because they mirrored my own. A kiss from Betsy would be… I couldn't fill in the blank. Would it be full of heat and passion? The way Betsy herself was? Or would it be painfully sweet and tender? The parts of herself she tried to hide revealed in the intimate moment?

I looked down at the tablet in my hand and noticed the transaction had gone through. With my pinned smile in place, I handed the man on the other side of the sales table his credit card. "Thank you and enjoy." He walked away with an autographed CD.

Jimmy sidled next to me. "Want me to take over?"

I set the tablet on the table. "Would you?"

He chuckled. "Doreen and I may be going on our twentieth wedding anniversary, but I still remember the thrill of the chase and the butterflies she let loose in my stomach." He shook his head, smiling. "What am I talking about? She still makes me feel that way." He picked up the tablet with the card reader plugged in.

"Anyway, I saw Betsy sneak back into the sanctuary a few minutes ago."

I clapped Jimmy on the shoulder. "Thanks, man."

He grinned at me before giving the person approaching the table his full attention.

There were two doors into the auditorium-like room from the lobby and two more on the sides of the opposite halls. I didn't want any of the people lingering in the lobby to follow me back to where we'd played, so I walked the deserted hall and slipped past one of the side doors.

Music met my ears and stilled my feet. All the lights had been turned off except a dimmed recess casting a glow at the very back of the stage. Betsy stood behind Jimmy's keyboard, the instrument unplugged from the amplifier so the notes she made it sing were only whispers in the large space. Low, tentative, her voice joined the melody, a mellifluous bridge crossing any obstacles to reach those who heard her. Reaching me.

I stood still lest any movement shatter the magic she spun. Listening to her made me ache in ways I'd never thought possible. The verse in Matthew about hiding one's light under a bushel came to mind. Her voice had the potential to be a lighthouse to someone in a dark storm, yet she refused to shine.

I couldn't make out the lyrics from where I stood, but I could hear the sadness and heartache in her tone. She painted strokes of emotion over my soul, moving my heart to the brink of falling off a great precipice.

My vision swam, and the final notes drifted away as if on a breeze.

"That was beautiful," I breathed. "You're beautiful." I stepped closer to the stage.

She lifted her face, her eyes wide. "You have a habit of catching me unawares."

I smiled softly. "I could say the same for you." I took another step forward. "You belong up there you know."

She shook her head, and her eyes pleaded with me not to press. To change the subject. Let her singing—or her refusal to sing, rather—drop. But I couldn't. If I wanted to explore these feelings I had for her—and I wanted to more than anything—then this was a conversation we had to have. A roadblock we had to clear in order to move forward.

I took a seat in the front row and motioned her to join me. "Come here." I watched her as she weaved her way between the microphone stands and descended the platform, my heart pinching as I willed her to trust me. No relationship ever succeeded without trust. If she couldn't trust me with what stood in the way of her doing what she obviously loved to do, then how could she ever trust me with her heart?

She lowered herself onto the seat next to mine, as tightly wound as a strand of her hair. I picked up her fingers and held them loosely in my hand. "Is this okay?"

She stared down at where our bodies connected, the

calluses on the tips of my fingers snagging on the silkiness of her skin. She swallowed and nodded, but her shoulders were held back as if by an invisible string.

I readjusted my hold on her hand and lazily traced circles around each of her knuckles in turn. Four beats for each knuckle. Four knuckles. Four-four time, each knuckle a complete measure. One, two, three, four. One, two, three, four. Slowly her shoulders lost their rigidity and she began to relax.

The metronome of my touch continued on the back of her hand. One, two, three, four. "Betsy." My fingers trailed the valley between her joints and rounded the base of the next. "There are so many things I want to say to you. To ask." I let a pause impregnate my silence. "But I don't have people close to you to question like you did," I teased.

A cheeky grin rounded her lips, and she flashed me a haughty look out of the corner of her eye.

"Did you get the answers you were looking for?" I whispered to her profile, my breath fanning the wisps of hair at her temple.

She turned her chin to face me, her long lashes rising to skim the bottom of her brows. "No," she murmured, her gaze searching mine. "I found the opposite."

My thumb froze, the beat of my heart going off rhythm.

"I found something better." With her free hand, she

reached over and covered my heart, sending it racing in a three-eight time signature. "I found you."

My tightly held control snapped in two. Every instinct, every desire I'd reined in was unleashed with those three soft-spoken words, and I couldn't get it back under control. Couldn't muster the desire to even try.

My mouth crashed down on top of Betsy's, an invitation to seek and explore to her heart's content. If she thought she'd discovered who I was, then I'd lay myself bare for her. I'd hold nothing back. She could have it all. All of me.

Every caress of my lips, mingled breath, shared touch—it was all a complex and yet simple-at-its-core overture. The promised beginning of a beautiful composition. The introduction to something even more substantial and lasting.

Could she feel my heart pounding beneath her palm? Hear all the things I longed to say expressed in my kiss? Know I'd do everything in my power to protect her from whatever had hurt her in the past? That I could easily fall in love with her? That I might have started to already?

Betsy met me touch for touch. She was fire, stoking the flames already burning through my veins. Every passionate challenge she'd ever flashed me through her gaze echoed in her kiss. I could imagine a future in which I told her I loved her and she replied with a competitive, *I love you more.* Where she goaded me with comments like, *that's all you've got?* until I was wrung dry giving her my everything.

I gentled my touch, my senses coming back to me. So much for patience. For waiting or talking first.

I kissed her again. Chaste and sweet compared to the urgency which had driven me to take her lips in the first place. I'd feel mortified except for the fact I hadn't been alone in my unbridled lack of control. Betsy had been right there with me. Matching me beat for beat.

I kissed her one final time then forced myself to lean back. As much as I loved losing myself in her touch, we still needed to talk.

Her hair was a halo of riotous, wild curls around her head, the product of my hands invading and tumbling through the silken mass. The disarray gave her an untamed, uninhibited look that made a feral growl climb its way up my throat.

Betsy's fingertips grazed her bottom lip, pulling my gaze to her red, plump mouth. I swallowed hard and forced my eyes to the ceiling, pulling deep breaths into my lungs.

"That was..." Betsy trailed off as if the rest of the sentence was out of her reach.

"I know." I looked back down at her and gave her a sheepish grin. "I think we might need to talk now more than ever."

"What do you want to talk about?" A thread of trepidation in a tapestry of composure.

I picked up her hand again, needing to touch her in

some way. To keep the connection between us. "First off, your rule."

"What about it?" She rested her temple against my upper arm.

"Well, do you still intend to keep it?"

She glanced up and smirked. "For you, I'll make an exception."

My chest squeezed. Would that be enough? Had she really come to a place of vulnerability, or would she be waiting for me to mess up in some way to justify her rule from the start?

"Why'd you establish that rule in the first place?" I asked, trying to keep my voice unaffected.

Betsy didn't answer for a long time. I started to wonder if she even would. Maybe she didn't think her heart or hurts were safe with me. I didn't know what else I could say or do to show her otherwise.

"About two years ago, this high school kid walked into my studio wanting to record a few original songs. He'd saved up his money from his part-time job, and I respected his hard work and dedication, so agreed to give him some pointers as well as recording and editing time." She gave a mirthless laugh. "The boy could charm the last two cents from a beggar and they'd thank him for it."

She paused, and I waited for her to continue in her own time.

"He really was impressive. Not just with his raw talent, but with his maturity. I'd never met any other eighteen-year-old that had such a solid plan for the future. Especially one interested in any of the arts."

She grew quiet, her mind seeming to return to that time and place.

"What happened?" I asked quietly.

"I introduced him to my sister. She was struggling with some of her friends, and I thought Wyatt could maybe help somehow since they went to the same school. They hit it off instantly and were practically inseparable after that." Her breath shuddered out of her. "Not much later, Wyatt received an opportunity to go to Nashville with the promise of something big on the horizon that would launch his music career. He got that phone call the same day Bella discovered she was pregnant."

My fingers tightened around Betsy's hand.

"My sister is a struggling teen mom raising her baby without a papi, while he's living the life of his dreams without a care in the world. The things he said to her before he left…" She shook her head, blinking back tears. "And I'm partly to blame. I should've seen his disloyal and self-seeking nature from the start. Should've protected my sister from him instead of being the one that fed her to that wolf in sheep's clothing."

I pressed my lips to the crown of her head. "I'm so sorry that happened."

She shrugged as if it didn't matter, but she was only lying to herself.

"That's why I made the rule." Her voice had gone flat.

Things fell into place to form a clearer picture. "And why you won't sing?"

She sat up straight and faced me. Looked me square in the eye. "I can never allow myself to be in a position where I am even tempted to turn my back on my family or walk away from who I am. Not for a dream or a passion or a purpose. I will not fall down any slippery slopes. Not if I keep my feet planted on firm ground."

Past the defiant tilt of her chin, I glimpsed fear in the back of her eyes. Sensed her pulling away, retreating back behind her walls once again.

"Do you think I will do that?" I tried to keep the hurt out of my voice. "That a career in music will change me and I'll become a man with a disreputable character?"

She didn't answer, just stared at me with her jaw locked in a stubborn line. Which was an answer in and of itself, wasn't it?

"You still don't really trust me, do you?" I pushed the words out on a pinched breath.

We had been so close. Right there. I could still taste her on my lips. Feel the ghost of her warmth where she'd placed her palm over my beating heart. But now it felt like I was clutching at air. Trying to hold on to something that I'd never really had to begin with.

Betsy blinked but otherwise sat impassive. The

passion and openness with which she'd kissed me minutes before had been erased, as if recounting how Wyatt had misused her sister had reminded her of all the reasons she'd walled herself away from anyone touching any piece of her heart in the first place. For now, there was no getting past that.

I stood up but didn't take my eyes off hers. "One day," I said quietly, "I hope you can see me the same way I see you." I gave her a sad smile and walked away.

19

Betsy

*T*he last week had been a rehearsed production, my body going through the motions while my mind and my heart watched from the wings. The band performed each night, somehow getting better with every song, the energy from the audiences pushing their talent and creativity to new heights.

I adjusted their EQs. Fixed their fades. But otherwise, I was removed. Numb. Impenetrable to the moving power of Asher's voice and the soul-searching depth of their music.

I should've felt safe. Secure. After all, hadn't I protected myself from surefire pain? Instead, all I felt was a deep sense of loss. Like something amazing had been at my fingertips and, instead of holding on, I'd shoved it away.

Asher's kiss stayed in my mind. That infuriating,

world-spinning kiss that had changed everything. If he hadn't touched me, then I wouldn't have known. I could've continued to live in blissful ignorance. But he'd barged through that door, opening me up to something I'd never thought possible.

His kiss had tasted like acceptance. Had felt like comfort in a way that dared me to be fully myself, no holds barred. There had been assurance, but with passion. Both sweet and spicy at the same time.

It had left me lightheaded and hungry for more.

Then my mind had cleared. He'd brought up my no-dating-musicians rule. My reasons for it. And everything my sister had gone through the last couple of years came crashing down like a tsunami, picking me up and pulling me back to a sea of bitterness and resentment.

Somehow, allowing myself to develop feelings for a musician felt disloyal to my sister. Especially because of the part I'd played in her broken heart. I couldn't risk my being with a singer and guitarist bringing Bella more pain. I hadn't done a good job of protecting her before, but I was determined not to make that same mistake a second time.

Why couldn't Asher see that? See that my wariness didn't come because of him (I *did* trust him...mostly), and stop pushing me to do or be more than I was willing. Why did me singing in front of people mean so much to him? It wasn't like he needed me up there with him. He could get a record deal with any label, either solo or with the band, if he wanted. So why was he making such a big deal about my refusal to sing in public?

I rubbed at my temples, then tapped my phone screen to check the time. Amanda and Peter should be here to pick me up any minute. I'd broached the subject of Jocelyn's engagement party on the drive from Las Vegas to Bakersfield. It just so happened that the party was on one of the few days the band had a break in their schedule. Amanda had said she'd detour on the way up to Malachi's ranch to pick me up and would drop me back off the next day with plenty of time to set up and do a thorough sound check before the concert.

Peter's old truck crawled through the campground's pebbled loop. I hopped off the weathered picnic table and slung the backpack I'd crammed with an extra change of clothes and my toothbrush over my shoulder.

The door to the bus opened behind me, and I turned my head enough to see Asher exit.

There went my secret getaway.

Peter's truck rolled to a stop and the engine died. I should've told Amanda to tell Peter to slow down enough that I could hop in the bed all fugitive-style, then gas it and get me as far away as fast as possible.

The way Asher was around me now—polite to a fault, studious but not engaging—made me feel like some sort of criminal. It would have been better if he'd yelled. Gotten so upset that he'd lost his temper. Maybe then some of the guilt weighing on my chest, pushing down until, at moments, I found it hard to breathe, would be lifted.

But he hadn't done that. He hadn't so much as raised his voice. The echo of his words, that I see him how he sees me, spoke through every look he gave me. Mostly, he seemed to be waiting. Like a steadfast sea anemone in a tidal pool. I couldn't tell if I was the rock he clung to or the crashing waves trying to rip him away. Maybe I was both. I didn't know. All that seemed certain was the longer I was forced to be so close to him while so desperately trying to keep my distance (I loathed that bus. Asher seemed to be right there every time I turned around—his smell, his presence, his voice), the more I wanted to toss my hands up in the air and recklessly throw myself into his arms and try to make the impossible happen—a relationship in which no one got hurt and everything worked out in the end.

Both the driver and passenger doors opened, and I sprinted toward the truck. "No need to get out. I'm ready. We can go."

Amanda gave me a quizzical look before ignoring me altogether. She stepped around me and smiled. Presumably to Asher, although I didn't turn around to find out.

"Nice to see you again, Asher," she said. "This is my fiancé, Peter Reynolds." She danced her fingers in Peter's direction.

Asher reached out and shook Peter's hand, no recognition on his face.

Interesting. Either Asher knew how to keep his cool around celebrities or he lived under a rock and had no idea that Peter was one of the most talked-about players in the NFL.

I parked myself in front of the truck's open door and smiled tightly. "Well, we should get going, don't you think? Long drive and all."

Amanda's long ponytail swept over one shoulder as she propped her chin on the other to stare at me. *What's wrong with you?* she mouthed.

I kept my brittle smile in place.

Asher rocked back on his heels. He gave me his lopsided grin, though it didn't hike as high on his cheek as usual. "Have a good time, Betsy. The bus won't be the same without you."

His eyes gleamed, and I blinked. Had it just been a trick of the light? The sun glinting of his irises, or had he…

That stinker!

His being right there every time I turned around, the brushing of our bodies when we needed to pass each other in the narrow aisle of the bus, the way his scent seemed to linger when I was trying to fall asleep. Those things hadn't been accidents at all. He'd planned every single one of them.

I spun on the ball of my foot and climbed into the

truck. A few minutes later, Amanda and Peter got in, shut the doors, then we drove away.

"What was that?" Amanda twisted in her seat to peer at me in the back of the cab.

"A campground. I'm sure you've seen one before." I reverted to sarcasm.

Her eyes narrowed. "As lovely as it was, I'm not talking about the campground. I'm talking about you and Asher. You texted and said not all musicians were bad and there were some worth getting to know better. Excuse me if I'm wrong, but we all thought that meant you'd finally gotten your head out of your butt and something romantic was happening with Asher." She faced forward again and crossed her arms over her chest.

Peter met my gaze in the rearview mirror. He didn't say anything but let go of the steering wheel with his right hand and comfortingly rested his palm on Amanda's knee.

We were all used to shocking things coming out of Amanda's mouth, but it had only been recently we'd learned that when she said those things it was in an effort to deflect our attention from the pain she was experiencing because of her autoimmune disease (which she'd named Delores because doctors had yet to name it with a proper diagnosis themselves).

"Delores giving you a hard time?" I asked gently.

She put her face closer to the side window. "Maybe.

But right now, one of my best friends, named Betsy, is too."

I pressed my lips together. I knew my friends would ask. Pester me even. But I was prepared. Maybe each of them had cracked and confessed their feelings during one of our sewing nights when they'd had trouble with love, but not me. They couldn't make me talk if I didn't want to.

I'd never been more wrong in my life. The CIA should hire Molly, Jocelyn, Nicole, and Amanda as their new interrogation officers. Waterboarding I could've handled, but being surrounded by their concern-filled faces while they relentlessly offered me support without the need for any explanation was becoming my undoing.

"We're here to celebrate Jocelyn and Malachi's engagement." I tried to make a final plea to logic, but my friends could sense my argument was struggling to stand, like a baby caribou surrounded my hungry wolves. "Not to talk about me."

Jocelyn nodded in agreement, then held up a staying finger. "But no one here will enjoy the party if we're all thinking and worrying about you. So, if you want to give me an engagement gift, spill."

I sighed and my shoulders slumped. Not only had I been shoved in the corner by Amanda, but everyone else had sensed something was wrong when multiple opportunities to say something sarcastic had arisen and I hadn't taken the bait.

I mean, sure, I would've been suspicious too if someone had left an opening about Drew's pink shirt making him look like he'd missed the last salmon run in Alaska and I hadn't commented on it.

"There's nothing to tell," I argued weakly.

Molly pursed her lips at me. "You know how I feel about lying."

"Do you like Asher?" Nicole asked point blank, obviously tired of my deflections.

I bit the inside of my lip.

Jocelyn perked up. "Silence is a yes. Next question."

"Did something happen between the two of you?" Nicole, being a mom, probably had a lot of experience getting the truth out of a reluctant witness.

The memory of Asher's kiss flashed through my mind. I kept myself still, pushing back my thoughts and feelings from showing on my face.

"Another yes!" Amanda bounced in her seat.

"Did you kiss?" Jocelyn beat Nicole to the question.

My nostrils flared.

Molly pointed at me. "They did! They kissed!"

Jocelyn reached forward and touched my knee. "What happened after your kiss?" She asked so tenderly that tears threatened to spring to my eyes.

"Nothing happened," I growled. "I came back to my senses is all."

"You shut him out you mean." Amanda dropped the sentence like a truth bomb. Everyone turned to stare at her. She held up her hands. "What? I did the same thing to Peter, so I'm able to recognize the behavior." She lowered her hands. "But, Bets, whatever reason you think you have to justify making the decision to push Asher away for his own good, being with you is *his* decision to make."

I averted my gaze.

"She didn't push him away for his sake like you did with Peter, Amanda." Nicole looked at me, calculating. "I'm not even sure she did it for herself."

This was the problem with best friends. Even if you didn't say anything, they still knew you enough to read you like an open book.

Nicole tapped her chin. "Who, though..."

"Her sister!" Molly brightened. "It all makes so much sense. I don't know why we didn't see it sooner."

My friends looked at me like they were stripping away the layers I'd put on to hide under.

"And you feel guilty..." Amanda spoke like she was working out an equation out loud.

"So you won't..." Jocelyn continued the thought.

Before I knew what was happening, Amanda had bolted out of her seat and snagged my phone, which had been lying on the table.

"What are you doing?" I half accused, half asked.

She tapped on the screen a few times, then held the cellular device to her ear.

"Who are you calling? And how do you know my password?" I wanted to make a grab for my phone, but I also didn't want to physically hurt Amanda unintentionally.

Amanda pulled the phone away from her ear and tapped the screen again. Ringing came from the speakers. She'd put the call on speaker phone so we all could hear.

"Hey, hermana. Que paso?"

She'd called my sister?

"Hi, Bella. This is Betsy's friend, Amanda. Actually, all of Betsy's friends are here."

The girls went around in a circle saying hi and introducing themselves.

"Don't tell them anything, Bella," I yelled like a hostage trying to warn someone about the bad guys in a movie.

She giggled over the line.

"We're actually calling because your emotionally-resistant sister has gone and developed feelings for a guy."

"Oh, please tell me it's the hot lead singer of the band she's touring with."

Amanda looked at me over the phone's screen, eyebrows raised.

"I told her to have some fun and live a little before she left, but I honestly didn't think she'd take my advice," Bella continued.

"So, you'd be happy if she started dating Asher North?" Amanda poked carefully.

My breath caught in my throat.

"Truthfully?" Bella sighed. "I'd be more than a little relieved."

"What?" I breathed out the word before I could stop the syllable from escaping.

"I feel guilty about everything that happened, and you seem…I don't know, stuck, I guess. You haven't seemed to move forward with either your personal or professional life, and I know that's my fault. If you dated, I think…I think I might be able to start to forgive myself."

Molly put one hand over her heart and dabbed the corner of her eye with the other.

I reached out my hand to Amanda, who placed the phone in my palm. "Bella, you have no reason to feel guilty about me. I'm the one who introduced you to Wyatt, so that blame is mine. Being with someone like Wyatt, even someone who loves music as much as he did—I don't want that to be a constant reminder and source of pain for you."

"Betsy, *you* love music that much."

I didn't answer because I didn't have a good argument to counter that.

"Do you really like this Asher guy?" she asked.

My friends stared at me. Nicole rolled her eyes when I didn't answer. "Silence means yes."

"Then you can't use me as an excuse. Not unless you want me to feel even more guilty than I already do."

I huffed a laugh. "Are you using guilt as a guilt trip?"

"Only if it's working," she teased.

"Brat."

She giggled again. "I learned from the best."

I ended the call and looked up. My friends beamed at me.

Jocelyn stood. "Now that that's settled, I'm taking the spotlight back." She smoothed out the wrinkles in her boho-chic dress. "I'm getting married!" she squealed.

I followed the girls outside to the back yard, where Malachi's grandmother had made his brother hang twinkle lights and his sister had arranged wildflowers in mason jars and set them on linen-covered tables. I pushed thoughts of Asher and what I'd do and say when I saw him again to the back of my mind. Tonight was for Jocelyn and Malachi.

20

Asher

*L*os Angeles traffic was going to give me a brain aneurism. It wasn't like I-5 didn't get as clogged as a frat house toilet after Oktoberfest farther south, but at least our bottlenecked lanes moved along like an infant already having learned to crawl. Here, with the Hollywood sign visible on the distant mountains to the east, we were at a standstill. Dave might as well have killed the engine to save on gas. It didn't look like we were going anywhere anytime soon.

"How about another game?" Tricia suggested.

I glanced back from the passenger seat and felt like I stared into three separate mirrors. Tricia at least looked to be fighting her frustration with the traffic by putting on a fake glow. Or maybe that was just the effects of being pregnant. Jimmy, Marcus, and Betsy, however, looked as fed up as I did.

"Let's play Highway Harmony." Tricia tried again when no one responded to her suggestion, much less with any sense of enthusiasm, feigned or otherwise.

"Never heard of it," Betsy mumbled.

Tricia's eyes flashed. I sat up straighter. What was the busybody up to?

As far as I knew, Betsy hadn't shared our moment in Las Vegas with anyone in the band, and I knew I hadn't. Then again, only someone completely oblivious wouldn't have noticed a shift between us. Tension crackled like a visible thing, the air charged around us. We'd become one of those plasma balls my fifth-grade teacher had had in the classroom. The ones that looked like they contained lightning inside a glass globe, but when you touched the surface, all those bright, shining currents shot out toward your hand.

"It's fun." Tricia's voice was overbright. "Someone starts singing a song and then a second person joins in by harmonizing."

Betsy's gaze flicked to me, the corners of her lips turned down.

Did she think I'd put Tricia up to this? While I fully wanted to encourage and support her to take the first step she was for some reason too scared to take, I'd come to accept that pushing her wasn't the way to do it. She'd only push back harder times ten. No, Betsy would have to come to her own realizations in her own time.

I just wished she'd let me close enough to see it when it happened.

"Betsy, you go first," Tricia pronounced.

"I really don't want—"

"Please. It will help me take my mind off things." She rubbed the side of her belly.

I couldn't tell if she was using the situation to manipulate Betsy or if she really was sincerely asking Betsy for a favor.

Betsy held Tricia's gaze for a few beats, then dipped her chin in agreement. After a moment of thinking, she began to sing.

"Amazing Grace, how sweet the sound, That saved a wretch like me!"

The timeless hymn, known and loved by many throughout the ages, filled the inside of the bus. Reached down and touched my spirit in the same way I imagined many had believed the waters of the pool of Bethesda were stirred.

Tricia hadn't named a person to step in to harmonize with Betsy, per the game's rules. Even if she had, I didn't think I'd have been able to stop myself from opening my mouth and joining my voice to Betsy's. She called out to me in ways I'd never heard before, and it was beyond my control to choose whether to respond.

When she started the second stanza, I came in under her. Lifted her up. Supported her in ways I'd longed to do, if only with my voice.

"I once was lost, but now I'm found; Was blind but now I see."

Our voices blended together in layers I hadn't thought possible. Like a chef finding the perfect balance of flavors with sweet, salty, acidic, and rich. I'd always suspected we'd sound good together, but even I hadn't been prepared for the harmony that danced around us in a perfect waltz.

Betsy's gaze had tangled with mine as soon as our perfectly pitched notes had floated out into the atmosphere. Current meeting current.

How could she not see? As well as our voices fitted together, we could be so much more. If only she wouldn't push me away. Would acknowledge the gift she'd been given. Trust that not every musician—me, her, if she'd ever accept that no matter how much she denied it, music was as much a part of her as anyone who took to the stage or was heard on the radio— would hurt those closest to them for the taste of a dream.

I wasn't alone in my growing feelings. Our kiss in Vegas had made that clear. But she would never truly be able to accept the two of us being together until she accepted all of herself first.

Tricia gasped and clutched the underside of her belly. "Ummm, guys?" She looked up at me, her eyes rounded in perfect circles. "I think my water just broke."

"What!?" Dave wrenched around to look behind

him, his elbow slamming into the steering wheel in the process.

Tricia bit her lip and nodded.

Marcus's face blanched. He looked back down at the phone in his hands.

"What do we do?" Jimmy's head whipped around, his voice panic-stricken. His gaze landed on me as if I'd have the answer.

"There's a hospital ten miles away." Marcus sounded like he was undergoing a second puberty. His voice was high and cracking. "We get off at the next exit and turn right."

I squinted out the windshield at the green road sign hanging in the distance over the interstate. The next exit was in half a mile, and we were in the lane beside the HOV lane. So all we had to do was cross three lanes of traffic on a major interstate that currently resembled a parking lot. No problem.

Betsy bolted out of her seat and lunged for the door.

"Where are you going?" Dave beat me to the question.

She paused, her fingers gripping the handle. "To help get Tricia to that hospital. Or do you want to deliver her baby right here in this Frankenstein bus?"

Dave just stared and swallowed hard.

Betsy opened the door and jumped down to the asphalt below. She sprinted to the car in the lane to our right. After she knocked on their window, the driver reluctantly lowered the glass. I could barely make out his reflection in the Chevy's side mirror but imagined the curiosity mixed with wariness there. At least, that would've been my reaction. One too many news stories on road rage and guns.

Betsy gestured wildly with her hands. The driver poked his head out of the lowered window and looked back at us. He nodded at something Betsy said, and then his back-up lights came on as she ran to the car in front of her. More pointing behind her, then waving her arm in front. The car started to creep forward, space widening just enough for Dave to wrench the wheel all the way to the right and crawl the bus's shoulder into it.

Tricia made a strangled noise followed by a low cry of pain. Marcus, Jimmy, and I all looked at each other for half a second before jumping out of the bus. Were we in Mini Coopers, we could *Italian Job* it in and out of this traffic. Instead, we were more like Sandra Bullock in *Two Weeks' Notice*—except with a woman about to have a baby!

I slid to a halt next to a minivan and frantically knocked on the window. The driver, a woman who looked to be about thirty with kids in car seats behind her, clutched the steering wheel until her knuckles turned white and refused to look or even acknowledge me.

"Ma'am," I tried again. "Ma'am. My friend is in labor. Can you pull forward as far as possible?"

Her gaze flicked to me and her chin dipped, but she didn't lower the window. As long as she made as much space as possible, that was all that mattered.

I ran to the next car.

The four of us played Frogger on I-5, weaving in and out of cars across the lanes and inching out as much space as possible. Dave worked the bus like threading a two-ton length of string through the eye of a needle. Once he made it to the right shoulder of the road, we scrambled back inside, and he hit the gas like the zombie apocalypse wanted Tricia's newborn's brains for breakfast.

Tricia was panting by the time Dave swung the bus into the emergency room drop-off area. I jumped out of the passenger side and ripped open the door for Tricia to exit. Betsy had an arm around Tricia's waist to support her. I held out my hand to help Tricia down the long step to the ground.

"She's having a baby!" Dave yelled behind me.

Tricia hissed, then groaned as her body tightened the second her feet hit the ground. Her grip on my hand could crush bones, but I'd gladly sacrifice being able to play the guitar again to wipe the pain etched into her face away.

After a moment, she was able to straighten and take slow steps forward. Dave raced out of the automatic doors with a wheelchair in front of him. He took the corner too quickly and the chair went up on one wheel, looking like it might tip over altogether.

Tricia squeezed my hand. "Don't let Dave push me."

I chuckled but dutifully took the handles from Dave once Tricia had taken a seat.

After answering the questions from the triage nurse —accompanied by several yells that she felt like she had to push—Tricia was whisked back to a room in Labor and Delivery, Betsy with her so she wouldn't have to be alone.

Jimmy sat in one of the waiting room chairs, phone to his ear as he talked with his wife. Marcus appeared to be texting, and Dave had disappeared, presumably to find coffee.

Me? I paced the floor. Was there someone I should call for Tricia? I had no idea how to get ahold of her husband. I should've asked for his information. Battalion name or something at least. He should know that his child was about to make her debut into the world.

I raked my fingers through my hair feeling helpless. I couldn't call Tricia's husband, but what about her mom? Though I didn't have her phone number either, I at least knew how to get it.

I dug my phone out of my pocket and dialed the church secretary. After explaining the situation, she gave me Tricia's mom's number. I called and explained again. Her mom grabbed her keys as soon as I said the word labor. She told me she'd make the Red Cross call to inform Tricia's husband. When I hung up, I stared at my phone. Was there anyone else I should contact? Anything else I could do?

The concert. The tour. I should call the rest of the venues and cancel. There was no way we'd continue without Tricia. I looked through my contacts to find the coordinator I'd been talking to for tonight's show.

"She did it."

Betsy's voice jerked my head up.

"She had a girl."

My phone slid into my back pocket. A baby girl.

Marcus stood. "Can we see her?"

Betsy nodded and led us down a long hall to a private room.

We all tiptoed in, the moment feeling sacred. Tricia sat propped up with pillows in the hospital bed, a precious bundle with a pink cap nestled in her arms.

"I'd like you to meet Melody Grace Williams."

"Aww. She's so cute and tiny." Jimmy spoke in baby talk.

"Do you want to hold her?" Tricia sat up straighter so she could safely transfer the newborn into Jimmy's waiting arms.

I approached the other side of the bed. "I called your mom. She's on her way."

Tricia dragged her gaze away from her daughter to reluctantly give me her attention. She looked tired and sweaty but happier than I'd ever seen her.

"Thank you."

"Of course." I awkwardly patted her shoulder. "I

was just about to call and cancel the rest of the concerts."

Her smile left her face. "Why would you do that?"

I glanced at Jimmy, Marcus, and Dave fussing over baby Melody. At Betsy hovering nearby like an avenging angel if any of them made a wrong move that would put Melody in jeopardy.

"Isn't it obvious?"

Tricia folded her arms, a stubborn jut coming to her chin. "You will *not* blow this opportunity because of me, you hear me?"

"Wow. That mom tone is pretty instantaneous, huh?" I tried to lighten the mood with a joke, but Tricia's glare didn't waver. I sighed. "True North isn't True North without you. We all play together or we don't play at all."

Her eyes narrowed. "You have two choices, Asher North. Either you go and sing your heart out tonight and impress the socks off that label rep without me, or you leave me no choice but to haul my sore and torn body out of this bed and sing beside you in a hospital gown while baring my backside to Dave at the drums."

"Tricia." I said her name, but what I really meant was *be reasonable*.

"Asher."

She could speak in hidden inflections too. I understood her *stop being stubborn* tone.

"Bottom line." Her voice had reverted to normal. "We're all here for you. Marcus, Jimmy, and I, we all see what you could become, and we were all willing to sacrifice for you to see it too. To reach your potential."

She held her hand out palm up, and I took it like she wanted me to.

"You and Betsy aren't all that different. She's scared to even step up to the starting line, but you're afraid of showing the world what you're truly made of and crossing that finish line in a blaze of glory. I don't know if it's because of your mom or what, but you've been holding back, Asher. We agreed to do this tour with you because we wanted to see you finally shine."

I shook my head. She was wrong. Wasn't she?

"You don't need me," she pressed. "And don't make any of our sacrifices be in vain." She patted my hand. "We love you. Let the world love you too."

I opened my mouth, but nothing came out. How was I supposed to respond to that?

Tricia turned from me and held out her arms to the quartet admiring Melody Grace. "Now give me my baby back and hit the road, Jacks."

Jimmy walked slowly back to her bedside and transferred the sleeping bundle. We said our goodbyes and filed out the door.

21

Betsy

here it was. Right where Tricia had said it would be.

I stared at the moleskin notebook lying beside Asher's leather-covered Bible. The same one he was nearly constantly scribbling in—equal parts writing, staring off into space, and then erasing and writing again. Guilt already started to weigh me down, and I hadn't even done anything yet. Wasn't even sure if I would. If not for Tricia, I wouldn't be standing there, looming like a bandit over treasure I planned to steal. But she'd begged me to find this notebook. To open it and read the page an old receipt kept bookmarked. Had argued that Asher was planning on sharing what was inside, but by then, it might be too late. Said if I cared about—no, *for*—Asher at all, I'd read what was written there. Then I'd know what to do next. No amount of questioning led Tricia to reveal either what I'd find or what she thought I should do. Just that I would *know*.

My fingers itched, the feeling traveling up my arms to scratch at the corners of my brain. I chewed on the inside edge of my bottom lip. Should I or shouldn't I?

I glanced around me, then grabbed the small book, hurrying to find the receipt being used as a place-holder. I quickly scanned the page.

It was a song.

Gravity pulled my body down to the seat behind me, and my eyes moved back up to the top of the page to read the lyrics.

In the deepest, in the quiet places
I can hear you, a song waiting to be written
You sing to me, a symphony, we'd be in perfect harmony
Our hearts beating as one

I close my eyes and listen
To you calling out to me
And pray that God grant you every blessing
And hope that someday I'll be counted as one,
A part of your destiny

So sing out, sing out

Let your heart ring out, ring out
Don't hold back, darling
Shine your light into the darkness
My shining star, you know who you are
I'll shine with you, if you want me to
Just say the word, I'm waiting to be heard

You sing to me, a symphony, we'd be in perfect harmony
Our hearts beating as one.

My eyes swam. The words floated in and out of focus as tears built then cascaded over the edge of my lids. I brushed the waterfall of moisture, like droplets clinging to a window in the rain, from my cheeks.

A strangled laugh pushed its way past my lips. Stupid, beautiful man.

How had we gotten here? From off limits to the precipice of yearning for unrestricted access? It felt like I'd been looking at him in a dimly lit room and someone had finally decided to turn a light on. How had I missed the depth of his gaze or the beautiful symmetry of his mind and spirit?

Maybe I was the stupid one. Too blinded by my misconceptions to see what was right in front of my face. To reach out and grab ahold of someone who saw more of me than I ever saw of myself.

I closed the notebook and tucked it under my arm.

I wasn't about to make the same mistake twice. I was willing to take that leap. For Asher and for myself.

I hurried out of the bus and made a beeline for Grace First's entrance. The church's sound guy had stopped by to offer a hand earlier, and if I was quick enough, maybe I could still catch him before he left. To put my plan into action, I'd need the help of everyone.

I pushed open the glass front door and barreled into the lobby like a bullet shot from a gun. One handled by a horrible marksman as, in my haste, I plowed into a solid chest, teetered, then ricocheted backward, my feet tangling together. Strong hands reached out and gripped my upper arms, steading me.

"For someone who makes it a point to let people know you don't fall for musicians, I sure have had to catch you from hitting the floor an awful lot."

My head snapped up at Asher's teasing voice near my ear.

He smiled, an outward display to accompany his attempt at humor and lightness. To put us on an even footing again after Vegas. But I saw the way sadness and regret weighed down the corners of his lips. There would never be even footing with us. Which could possibly explain why I was always tripping and finding myself in his arms. He skewed my equilibrium. Made me feel unbalanced in the most thrilling way possible.

His head tilted and his brows furrowed. "Is everything okay?"

I tried to school my features, but he could always see past my defenses. While I could fool everyone else, I'd never been able to fool Asher.

I could tell him. Right here, right now. Tell him that none of the things I thought were keeping us apart mattered. That I trusted him. Apologize for ever thinking he would turn out to be anything like Wyatt or other guys I'd worked with in the past at the studio. Tell him that my sister wasn't a road block at all but that she wanted us to be together.

I could. But would he believe me? Words could be pretty. His lyrics and compositions proved that. But he could've told me he was trustworthy until he was blue in the face. It wasn't until I could see the truth in his actions that I began to believe it.

Asher deserved my truth in action as well. I wouldn't just tell him how I felt. I'd show him.

I smiled up at him. "I'm fine. Just in a hurry to catch the PA guy. I need to ask him something before he leaves." I made to walk away, but Asher caught me by the hand.

"Betsy, I..."

His gaze burned as he looked at me. My blood heated in my veins.

Just when I was about to show him my feelings in a different way than planned—sear the truth to his lips with a kiss—the fire banked in his eyes and he dropped my hand.

"Never mind." He shook his head.

I bit my tongue to keep from saying anything, then turned on my heel in search of everyone I'd need as an accomplice to pull off my plan.

Hours later, the fifteen hundred seats in the worship center full, Asher took to the stage in a pair of faded jeans and a button-up shirt with the sleeves rolled to his elbows. I watched from behind the wall that hid the waiting area from the audience's view. His natural charisma immediately pulled everyone in, making them fall in love with him instantly.

I peered around the corner of the wall and squinted to see out into the crowd. With the house lights dimmed and the spotlights shining onto the stage, it was difficult to see past the first row. Was the representative from the recording label here? Was he sitting somewhere among the shadows? Perhaps the man with the mustache sitting on the end? Or the lady in the lace top?

Asher played the introduction of the first song on his guitar, plucking the strings. It was a number that Tricia and the rest of the band members only sang a minimal backup to. They'd decided to change some of the set arrangements to accommodate not having a female vocal.

Asher's voice rang out, strong and melodious, growing as the song crescendoed, then pooling sweetly and falling gently as the emotion of the piece evicted a contemplative response. He held the final note until it softly dissipated over the audience's heads.

Applause followed, some people even rising to their feet.

I gripped the microphone in my hand, wishing I'd rubbed my damp palm along the side of my pants to dry first. My heart pounded in my ears. Jimmy looked over at me as the crowd began to die down. Before Asher could announce the next song, I dipped my chin. Jimmy nodded back, then set his fingers on the keys of his keyboard and played the opening measures of Asher's hidden song.

My gaze was focused on Asher, so I knew the exact moment the notes clicked in his brain. He jerked, then pivoted. *What are you doing?* he mouthed. Indecision warred on his face. He couldn't decide if he should stop Jimmy and make some kind of joke to mask the mistake for the crowd or do nothing.

I raised the microphone to my lips and took a steadying breath. "In the deepest, in the quiet places; I can hear you, a song waiting to be written."

Asher's gaze zeroed in on me like a missile locking on to a target. His eyes rounded.

"You sing to me, a symphony, we'd be in perfect harmony." I nodded toward him and smiled softly as I sang.

Wonder filled his face. He looked stunned. Trans-fixed. There was so much I wanted to say to him. That I wanted him to know. I hoped he could hear my heart through the words he himself had written. See that I wouldn't hide anymore—not from him or myself. I hoped my voice projected so that over a thousand people could hear my declaration to Asher. That through this song, he'd know I was falling in love with him.

The part of the song written as a duet approached. Asher gripped the microphone and joined his voice with mine, his gaze never straying from my eyes. His hand lifted, and he reached out, palm up, inviting me to his side.

I didn't hesitate. Not this time. I stepped out onto the stage, Asher reeling me in with the love pouring out of his gaze and the words his heart had bled onto the page. When I reached him, he interlocked our fingers, and we sang the lyrics to each other, the audience forgotten. While the crowd looked on, we cocooned ourselves in the music. In each other. Every chord was a promise. Each note a declaration. This moment was a chorus we'd be coming back to again and again.

The song ended and Asher swung his guitar to his back, then swallowed me in his embrace. The crowd's applause hammered in my ears along with the beat of my own heart.

Asher pulled away far enough to cradle my face in his hands. He searched my eyes in that way of his, then grinned so brightly my pulse tripped over itself.

"You're amazing." He had to near-shout to be heard over the ovation. He leaned down and claimed my lips just as he'd already claimed my heart.

Whistles accompanied the clapping. Instead of feeling embarrassed and pulling away, I rose up on my toes and offered him something I'd hidden away most of my life—all of me.

EPILOGUE

*P*eter held Amanda close as they twirled around the parquet dance floor, the fullness of her wedding dress billowing out behind her as he led her in a spin, then pulled her back in to his chest. He gazed down into her face, love evident in the gentle way he held her. In the way his gaze could be a physical thing, reaching out and caressing her with featherlight touches.

Before, I might have rolled my eyes. Happy for my friends but slightly nauseated at the lovey-dovey nonsense that turned their brains into mush in each other's company. You see, I didn't understand. The power of love. Not to make people illogical nincompoops, but to transform. To help shape us into the best versions of ourselves. Versions we were too blinded to even see were possible.

I looked to my right. Asher sat perched on a stool,

guitar propped on his bent leg, his fingers strumming the six strings as we sang together the song Amanda felt embodied her and Peter's journey to each other, the broken road that made their paths cross a second time and launched them on their journey to forever and always.

As Asher strummed the final chord, Peter dipped Amanda on the dance floor, kissing her to a riotous round of applause and whistles from everyone at the reception. I laughed and clapped along. Asher grinned, then set his guitar back inside its case. The DJ in the corner put on a new track, and Old Blue Eyes crooned through the speakers about the way she looked tonight. Other couples joined the newlyweds on the rented dance floor square, swaying to the classic love song.

Asher held out his hand to me. "May I?"

My palm slid across his. "You may."

He led me to an open spot amid the other pairs dancing, then pulled me close, our bodies flush together. I rested my head on his shoulder as we swayed side to side. His thumb caressed the curve of my waist over the blush-pink bridesmaid dress I wore. With his mouth near my ear, he sang along with Sinatra, a private serenade just for me.

I pressed my palm flat against his chest. I never tired of hearing the beat of his heart. It was a metronome that provided a steady, consistent rhythm that instantly grounded my own sometimes erratic pulse. I slid my thumb and forefinger along opposite sides of his lapels and tugged. His chuckle rumbled beneath my cheek, making me smile.

"Our first gig as wedding singers." I leaned back to look up into his eyes. "If things don't end up working out with Capitol Christian Music Group, at least we know we have a Plan B to fall back on."

He grinned. "Which one of us is Adam Sandler in this scenario?"

I fingered the closely cropped hair at the base of his neck. "I guess that depends on which of us would look better with a curly mullet."

He winced before taking one of my spiral curls between his fingers. "It would be a tragedy to cut your hair, so I guess I'll have to take one for the team."

I laughed and shook my head. "Seriously though. Are you ready to do this at least two more times? Nicole's getting married in a few weeks, and Jocelyn and Malachi are tying the knot in the fall. Both have asked us to sing at least one song either in the ceremony or at the reception."

Asher raised his face and looked around the room, then gripped my hand and pulled me through the dancers toward the exit.

"Where are we going?" I whisper-shouted in hopes he could hear me without disturbing anyone else.

He tugged me through a door, guiding me to step sideways with a hand to my hip, then pushed me up against the wall, stepping into the space in front of me. One hand still on my hip, he cradled my neck with the other as he bent his head to look me straight in the eye.

"At least *three* weddings."

"What?" My brain scattered at his proximity. All I could do was breathe in the heady scent of the cologne he wore and wonder why he was wasting his breath talking when we could be kissing instead. We hadn't had much privacy, what with the tour, wedding preparations, and talks with the music label. I wouldn't have minded experiencing what kissing without an audience was like.

One corner of his lips tilted as if he could read my thoughts. His grip on my neck tightened enough for me to know I wasn't the only one whose brain had gone in that direction.

I lifted my chin, an invitation to my lips.

Asher's pupils dilated. His muscles tensed, but he didn't lean forward. He didn't move at all.

"Nicole and Drew. Jocelyn and Malachi," he said slowly, matter-of-factly. He waited a beat. "And then you and I."

I gasped, mouth open. He took that moment to swoop in, his lips crashing down on mine. He stole whatever knee-jerk reaction I would've had with his kiss and swallowed it down. Silenced my quips and let the rest of his arguments and persuasions be spoken with the fierceness of his kiss.

"I'm not proposing right now," he said as he gasped

for breath, his lips never leaving contact with my skin. "I'm just making you aware of my intentions."

My hands found their way inside his suit jacket, and I fisted the material of his shirt at his lower back. "Well, right now my intentions are to keep kissing you. Then I intend to keep trusting you. To always be open and honest. To not hide but stand by your side day in and day out. I intend to never stop loving you." I pulled him closer so that I was sandwiched between the wall and the length of his body. "Beat that, Asher North."

He laughed, shook his head, then kissed me again, more than happy to take my bait and rise to my challenge.